380L

D1283890

WITHDRAWN

Does a Great Job

by Chris "Elio" Eliopoulos

STONE ARCH BOOKS
A CAPSTONE IMPRINT

Mr. Puzzle is published by Stone Arch Books,
a Capstone imprint
1710 Roe Crest Drive
North Mankato, Minnesota 56003
www.capstonepub.com

Cataloging-in-Publication Data is available
on the Library of Congress website.

ISBN (library binding): 978-1-4342-6025-3

Ashley C. Andersen Zantop - PUBLISHER
Donald Lemke - EDITOR
Michael Dahl - EDITORIAL DIRECTOR
Brann Garvey - SENIOR DESIGNER
Heather Kindseth - CREATIVE DIRECTOR
Bob Lentz - ART DIRECTOR

Printed in China by Nordica.
0413/CA21300512
032013   007226NORDF13

MR. PUZZLE

Does a Great Job

CAMILLUS

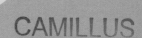

BY CHRIS "ELIO" ELIOPOULOS

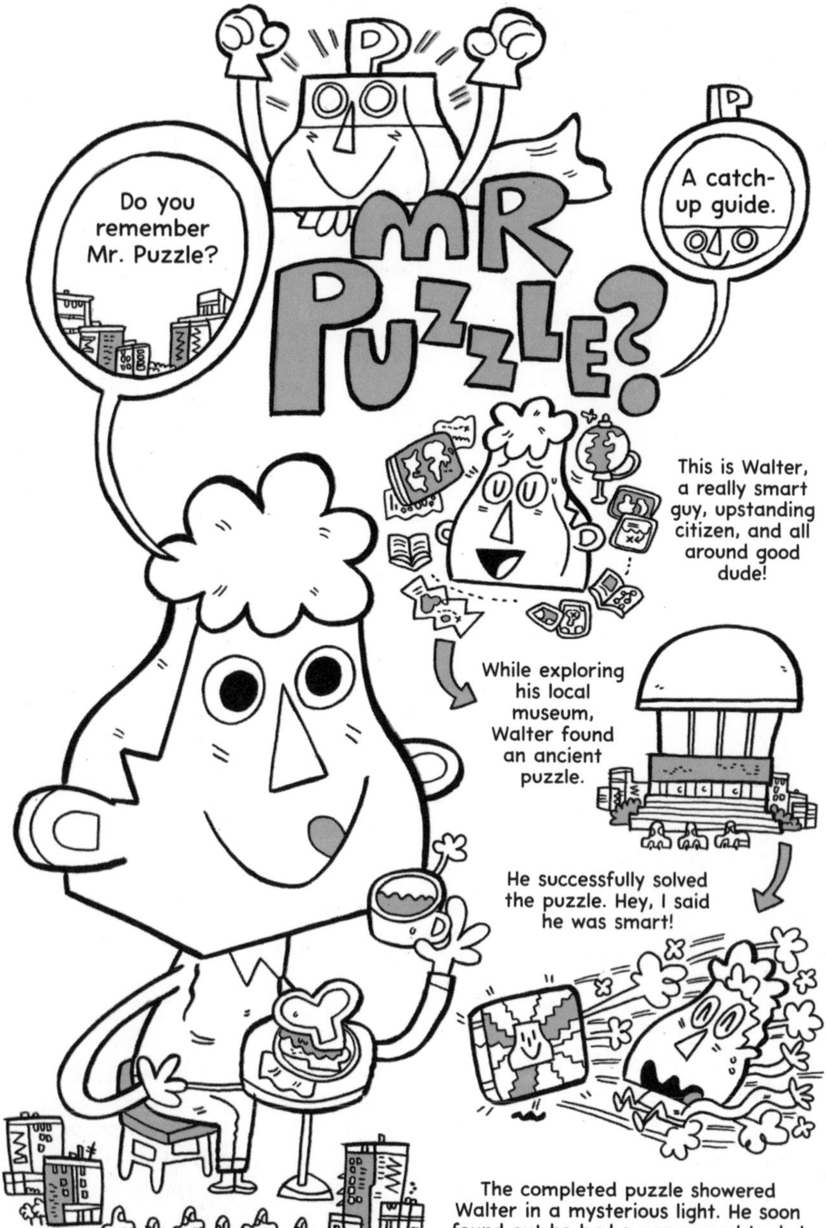
Do you remember Mr. Puzzle?
MR PUZZLE?
A catch-up guide.
This is Walter, a really smart guy, upstanding citizen, and all around good dude!
While exploring his local museum, Walter found an ancient puzzle.
He successfully solved the puzzle. Hey, I said he was smart!
The completed puzzle showered Walter in a mysterious light. He soon found out he had superpowers! Lucky!

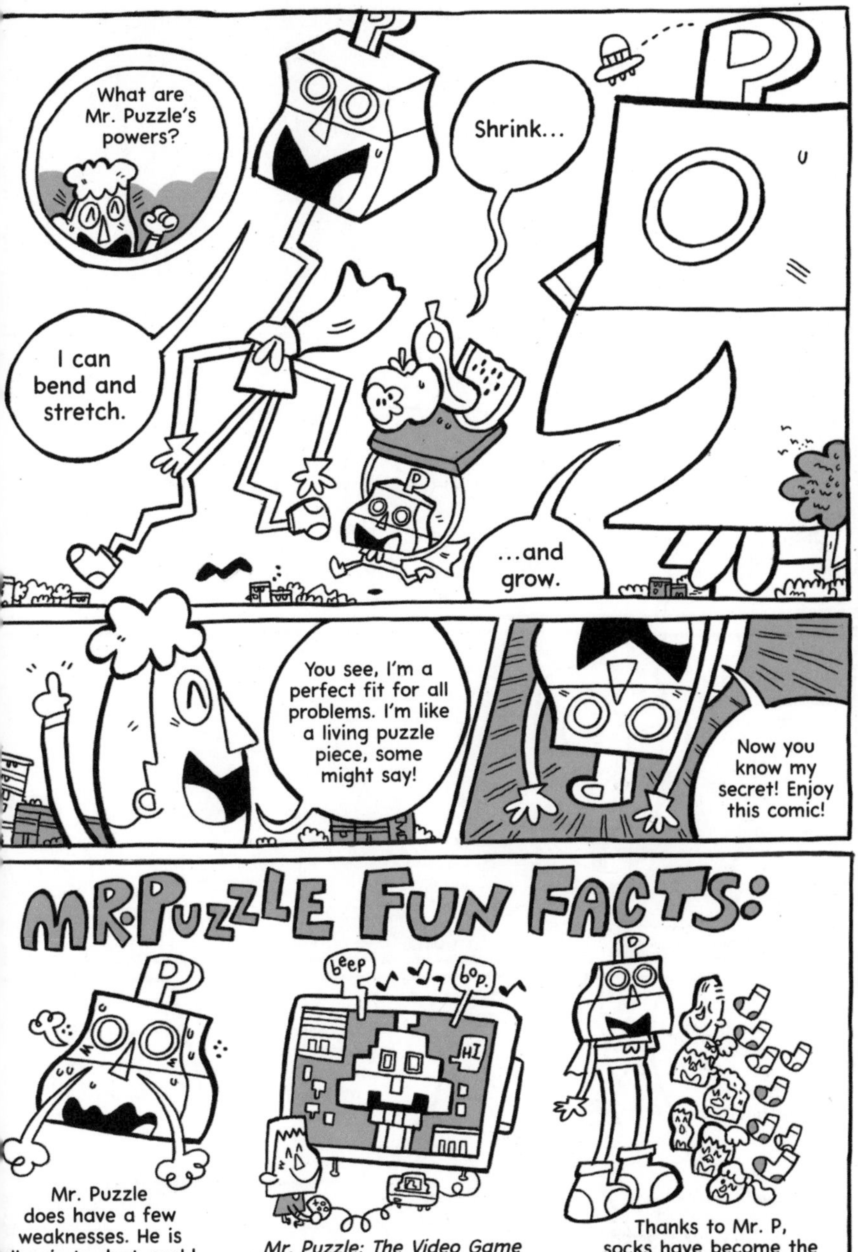
What are Mr. Puzzle's powers?
I can bend and stretch.
Shrink...
...and grow.
You see, I'm a perfect fit for all problems. I'm like a living puzzle piece, some might say!
Now you know my secret! Enjoy this comic!
MR. PUZZLE FUN FACTS:
Mr. Puzzle does have a few weaknesses. He is allergic to dust, mold, and some types of seasonal pollens.
beep
bop.
HI
Mr. Puzzle: The Video Game is currently the highest selling action/adventure game today.
Thanks to Mr. P, socks have become the new fashion statement. Everyone is wearing them!

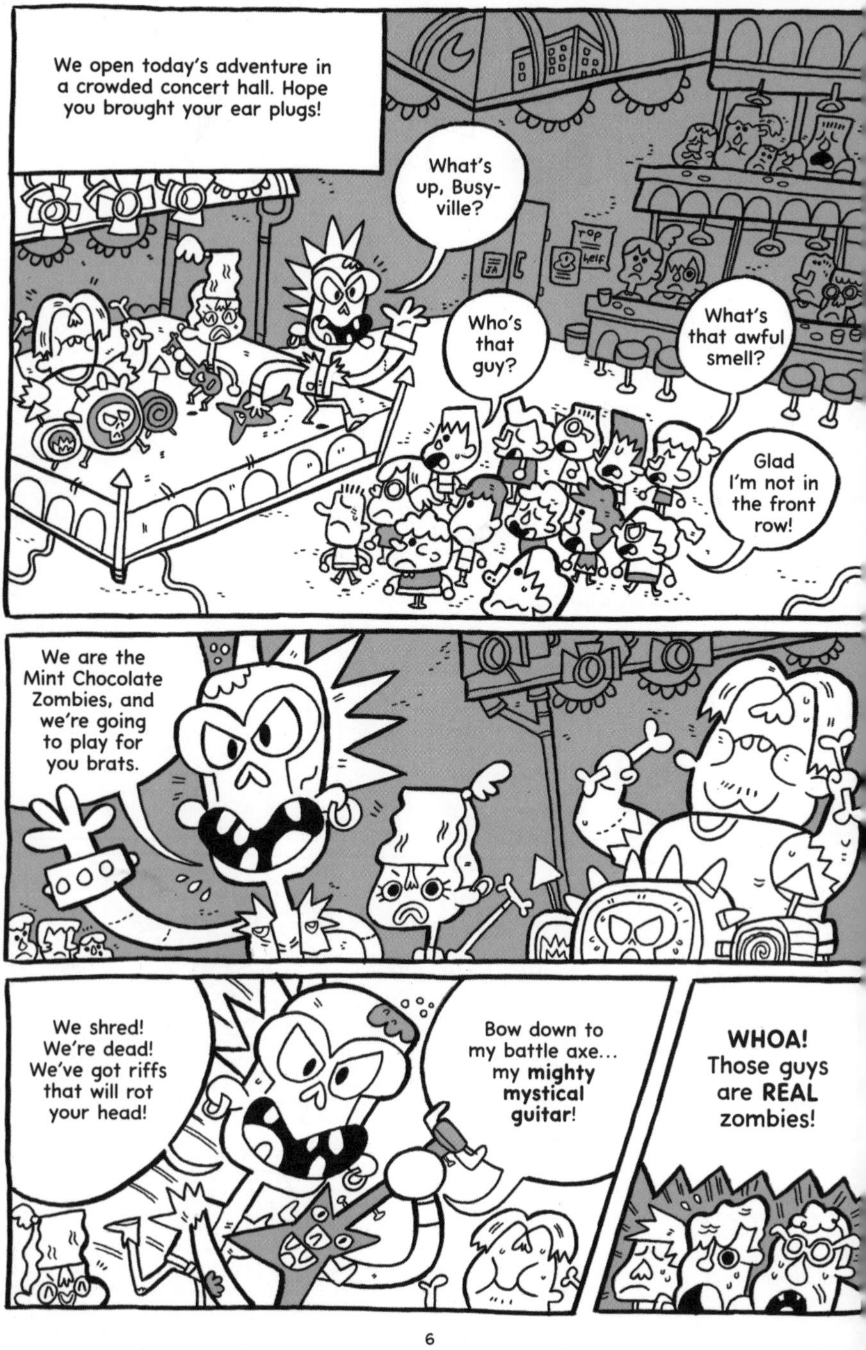
We open today's adventure in a crowded concert hall. Hope you brought your ear plugs!
What's up, Busy-ville?
Who's that guy?
What's that awful smell?
Glad I'm not in the front row!
We are the Mint Chocolate Zombies, and we're going to play for you brats.
We shred! We're dead! We've got riffs that will rot your head!
Bow down to my battle axe... my **mighty mystical guitar**!
WHOA! Those guys are **REAL** zombies!

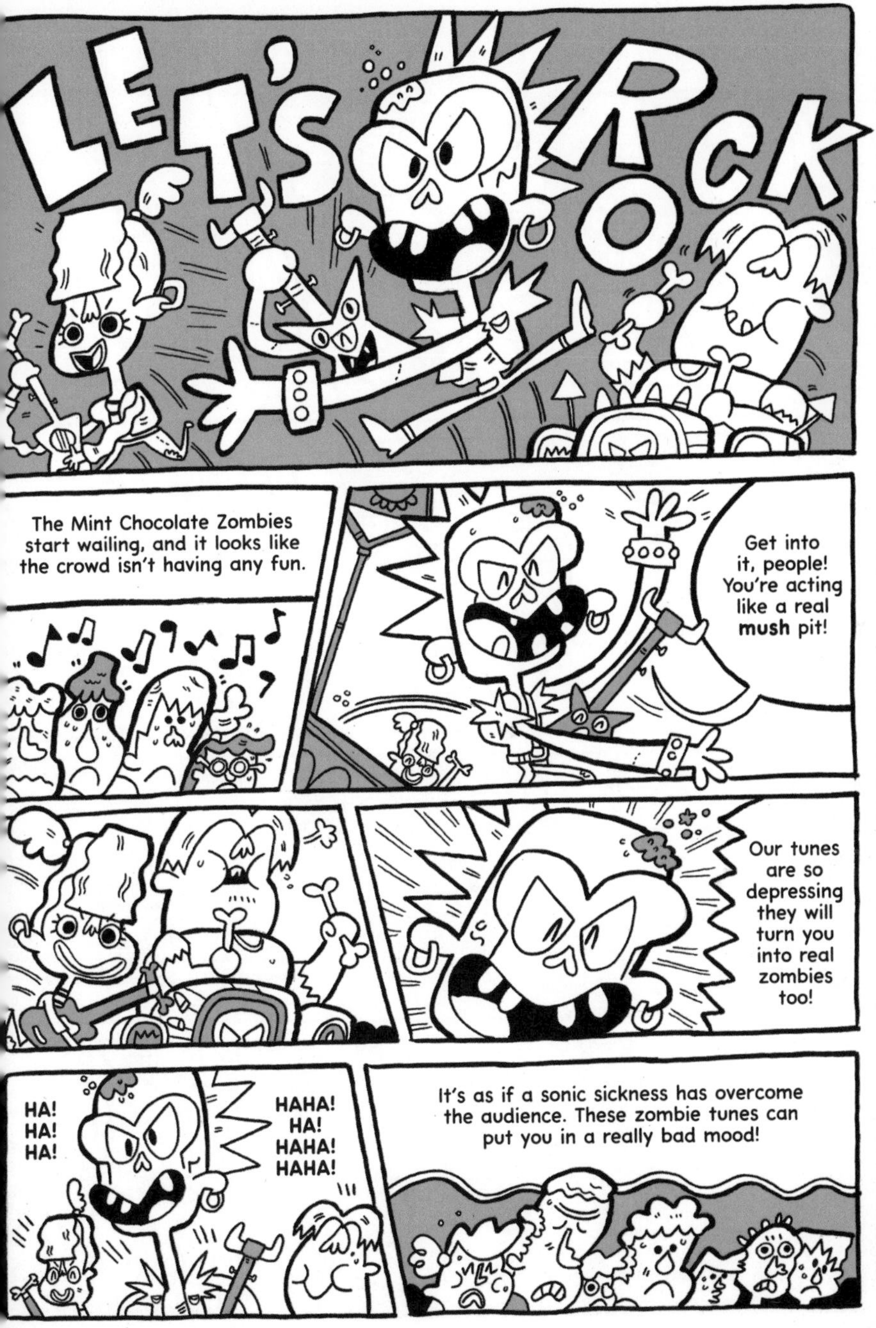
LET'S ROCK
The Mint Chocolate Zombies start wailing, and it looks like the crowd isn't having any fun.
Get into it, people! You're acting like a real **mush** pit!
Our tunes are so depressing they will turn you into real zombies too!
HA! HA! HA!
HAHA! HA! HAHA! HAHA!
It's as if a sonic sickness has overcome the audience. These zombie tunes can put you in a really bad mood!

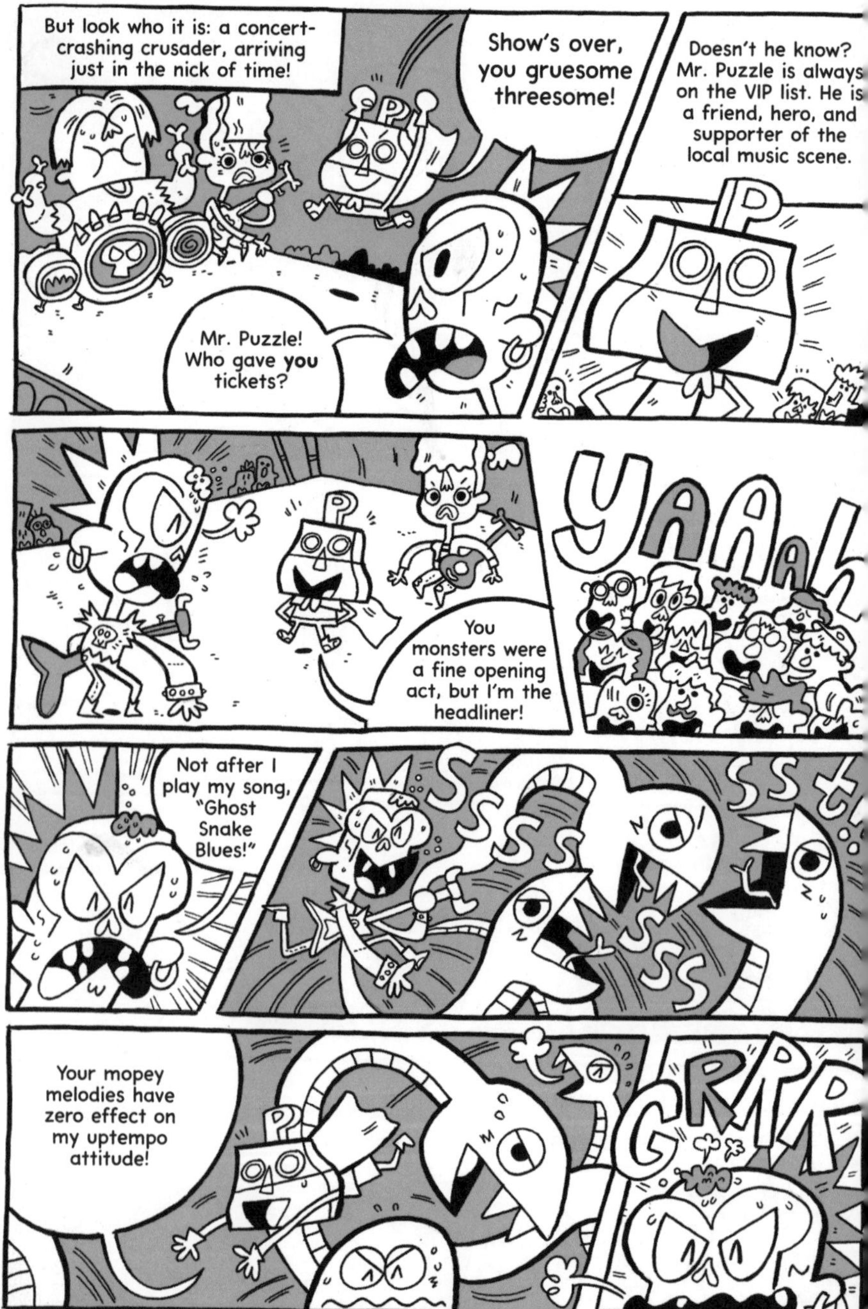

But look who it is: a concert-crashing crusader, arriving just in the nick of time!
Show's over, you gruesome threesome!
Mr. Puzzle! Who gave you tickets?
Doesn't he know? Mr. Puzzle is always on the VIP list. He is a friend, hero, and supporter of the local music scene.
You monsters were a fine opening act, but I'm the headliner!
Not after I play my song, "Ghost Snake Blues!"
Your mopey melodies have zero effect on my uptempo attitude!

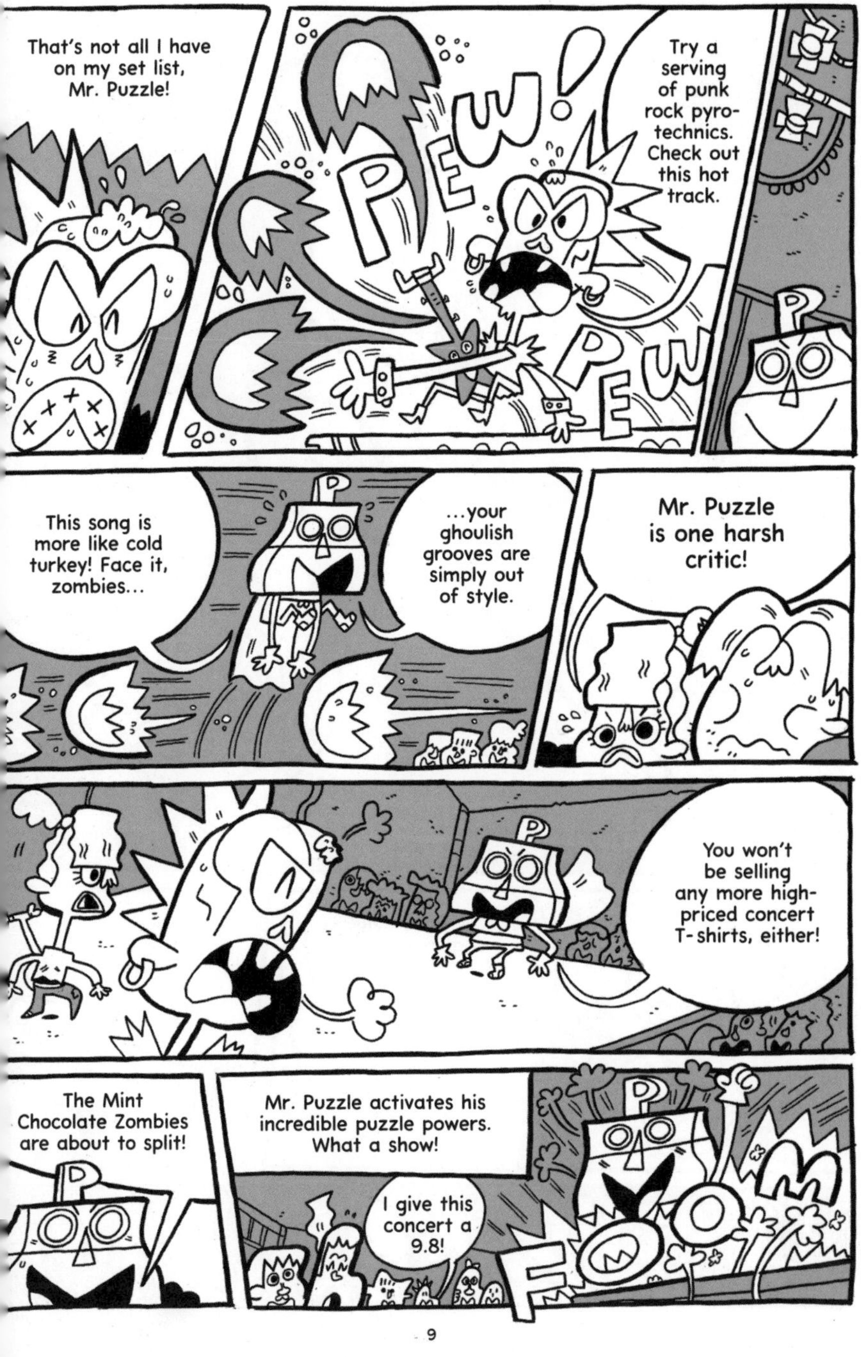
That's not all I have on my set list, Mr. Puzzle!
PEW!
Try a serving of punk rock pyro-technics. Check out this hot track.
PEW
This song is more like cold turkey! Face it, zombies...
...your ghoulish grooves are simply out of style.
Mr. Puzzle is one harsh critic!
You won't be selling any more high-priced concert T-shirts, either!
The Mint Chocolate Zombies are about to split!
Mr. Puzzle activates his incredible puzzle powers. What a show!
I give this concert a 9.8!
FOOOM

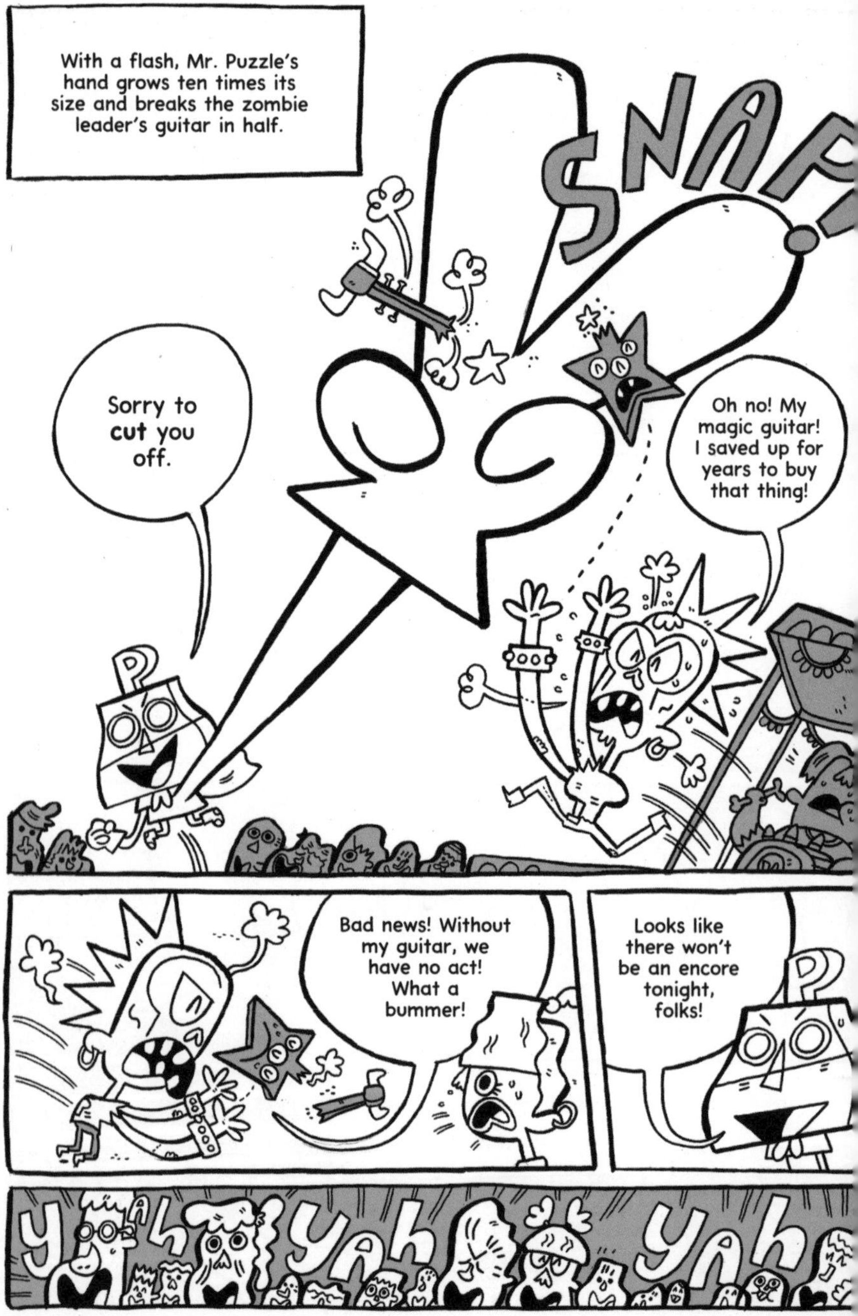

With a flash, Mr. Puzzle's hand grows ten times its size and breaks the zombie leader's guitar in half.
SNAP!
Sorry to **cut** you off.
Oh no! My magic guitar! I saved up for years to buy that thing!
Bad news! Without my guitar, we have no act! What a bummer!
Looks like there won't be an encore tonight, folks!
YAH YAH YAH

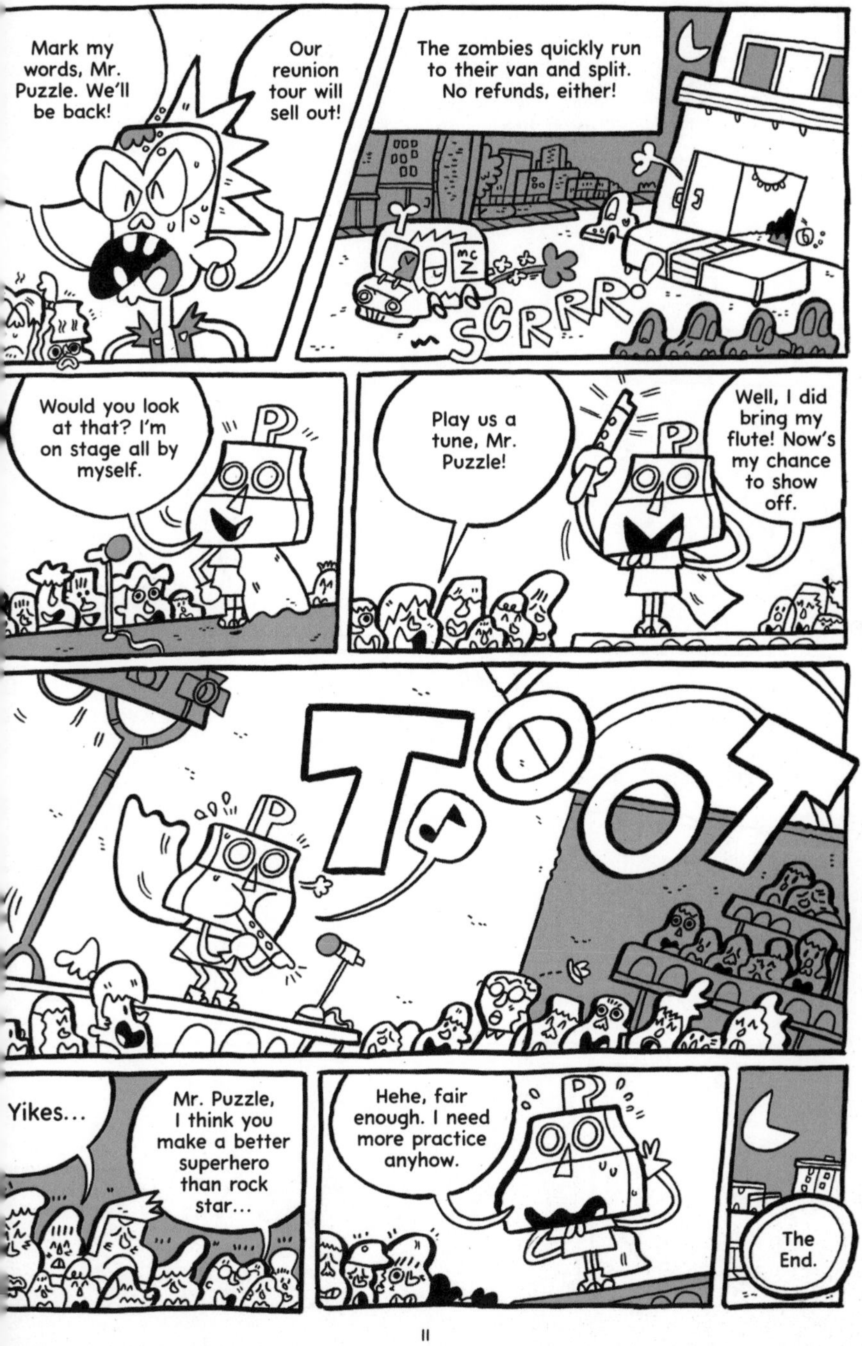
Mark my words, Mr. Puzzle. We'll be back!
Our reunion tour will sell out!
The zombies quickly run to their van and split. No refunds, either!
SCRRR!
Would you look at that? I'm on stage all by myself.
Play us a tune, Mr. Puzzle!
Well, I did bring my flute! Now's my chance to show off.
TOOT
Yikes...
Mr. Puzzle, I think you make a better superhero than rock star...
Hehe, fair enough. I need more practice anyhow.
The End.

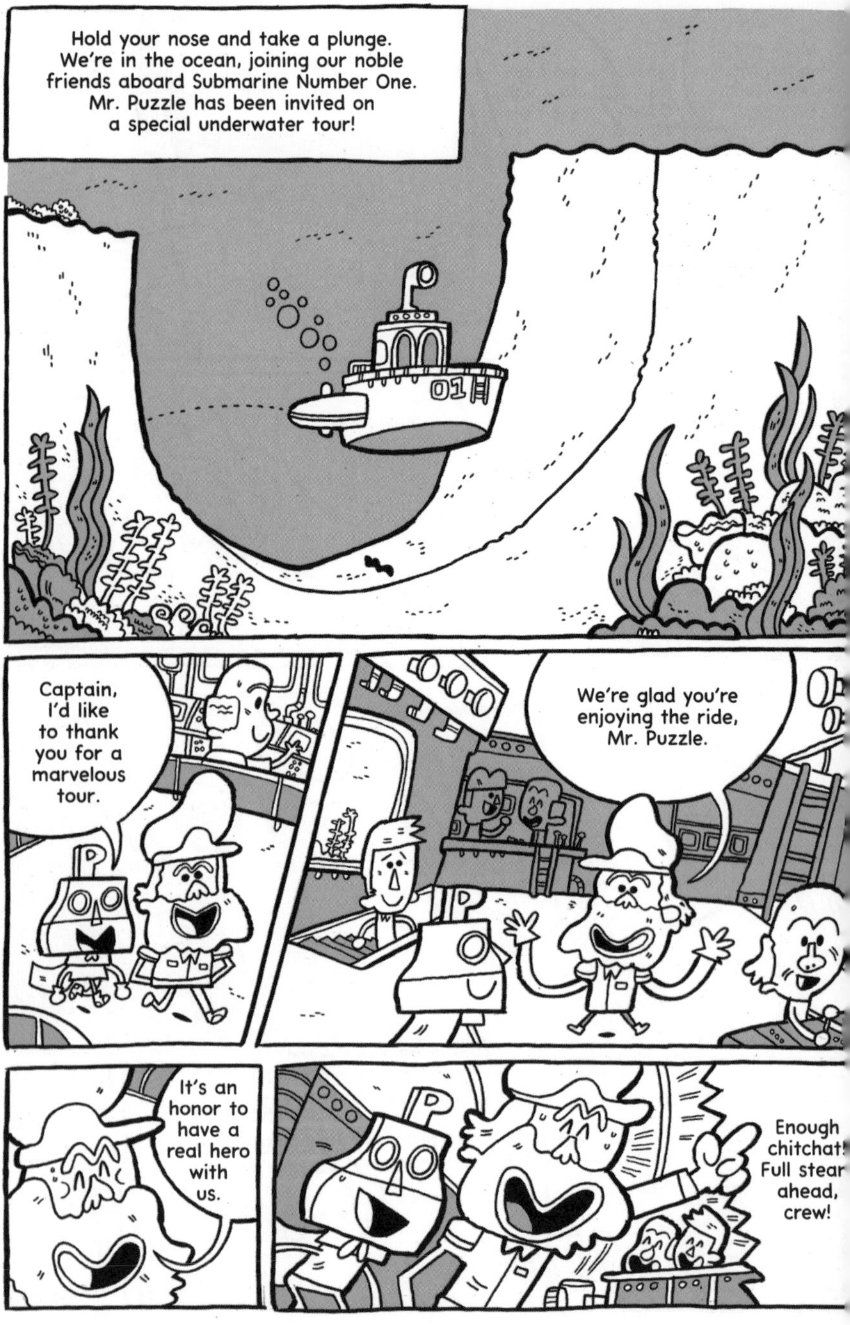
Hold your nose and take a plunge. We're in the ocean, joining our noble friends aboard Submarine Number One. Mr. Puzzle has been invited on a special underwater tour!
01
Captain, I'd like to thank you for a marvelous tour.
We're glad you're enjoying the ride, Mr. Puzzle.
It's an honor to have a real hero with us.
Enough chitchat! Full stear ahead, crew!

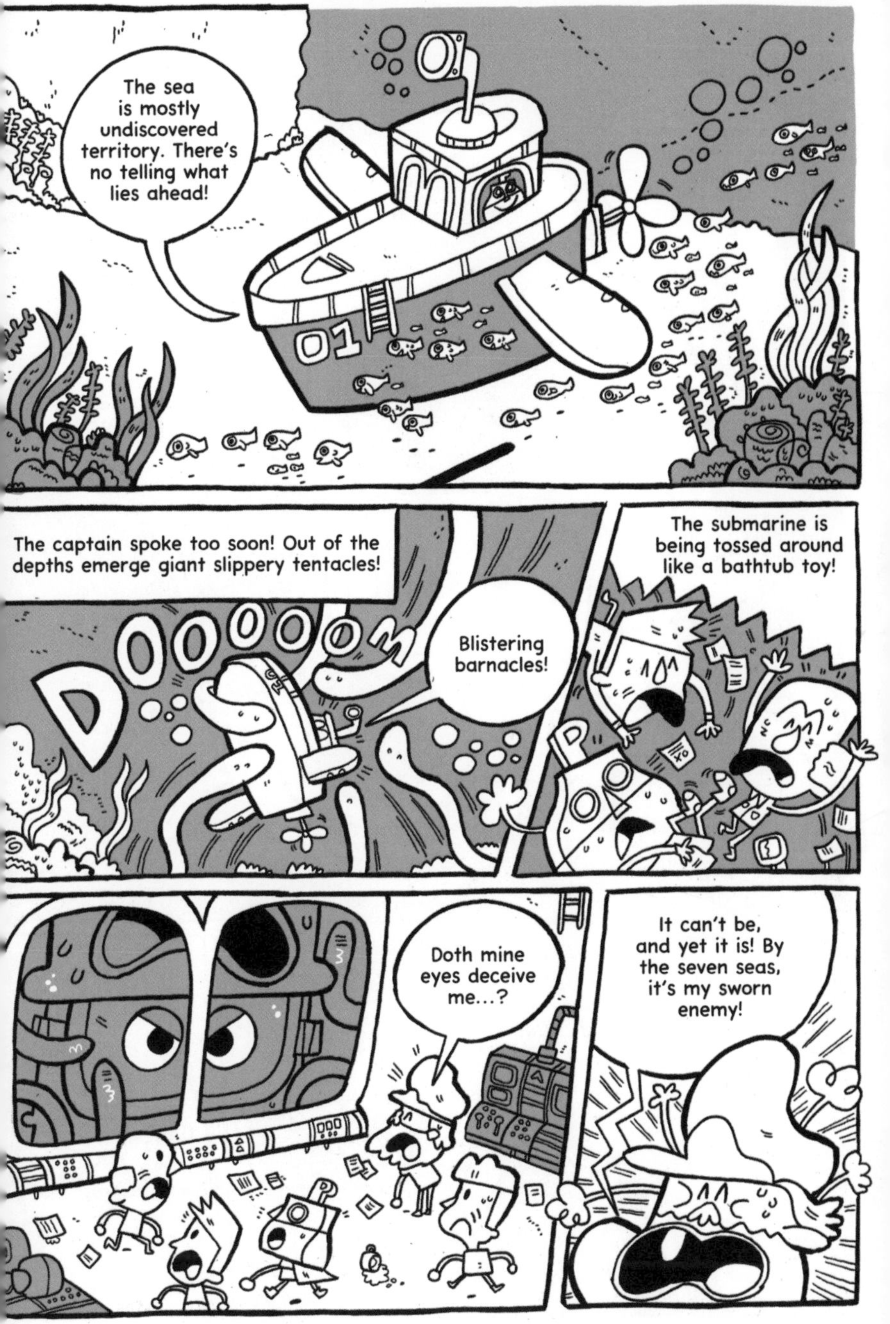
The sea is mostly undiscovered territory. There's no telling what lies ahead!
01
The captain spoke too soon! Out of the depths emerge giant slippery tentacles!
DOOOOOOM
Blistering barnacles!
The submarine is being tossed around like a bathtub toy!
Doth mine eyes deceive me...?
It can't be, and yet it is! By the seven seas, it's my sworn enemy!

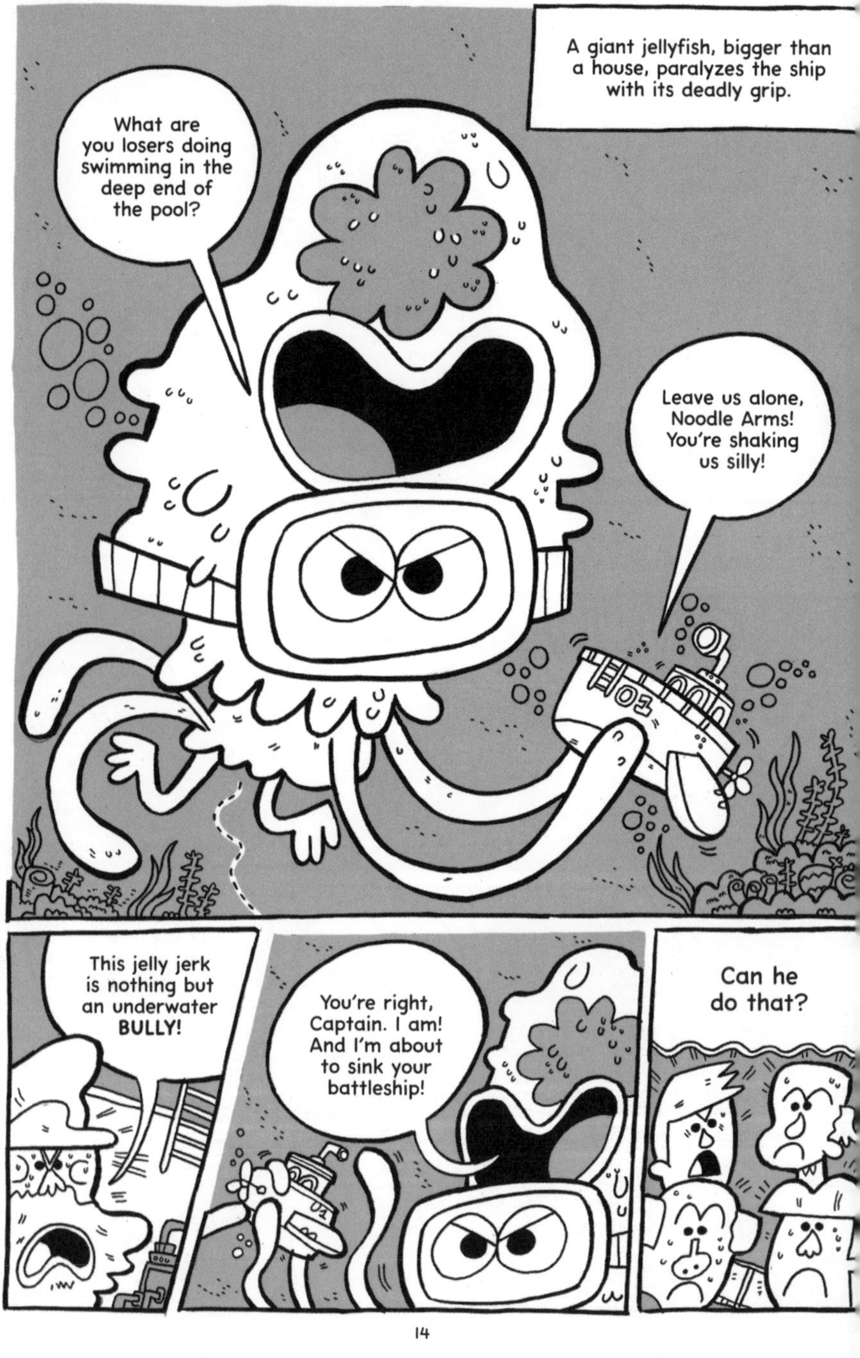
A giant jellyfish, bigger than a house, paralyzes the ship with its deadly grip.
What are you losers doing swimming in the deep end of the pool?
Leave us alone, Noodle Arms! You're shaking us silly!
This jelly jerk is nothing but an underwater **BULLY!**
You're right, Captain. I am! And I'm about to sink your battleship!
Can he do that?

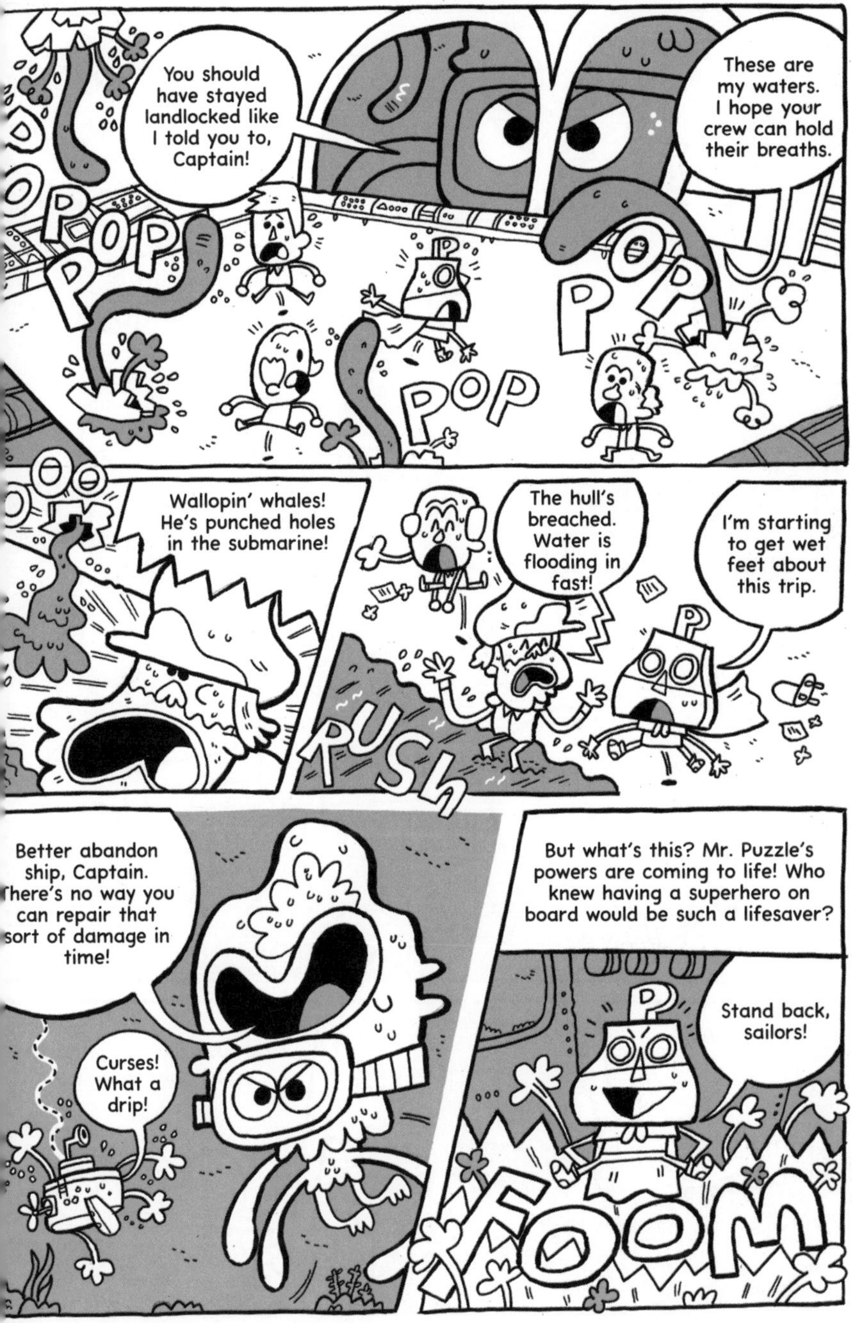
You should have stayed landlocked like I told you to, Captain!
These are my waters. I hope your crew can hold their breaths.
POP
POP
POP
POP
POP
Wallopin' whales! He's punched holes in the submarine!
The hull's breached. Water is flooding in fast!
I'm starting to get wet feet about this trip.
RUSH
Better abandon ship, Captain. There's no way you can repair that sort of damage in time!
Curses! What a drip!
But what's this? Mr. Puzzle's powers are coming to life! Who knew having a superhero on board would be such a lifesaver?
Stand back, sailors!
FOOM

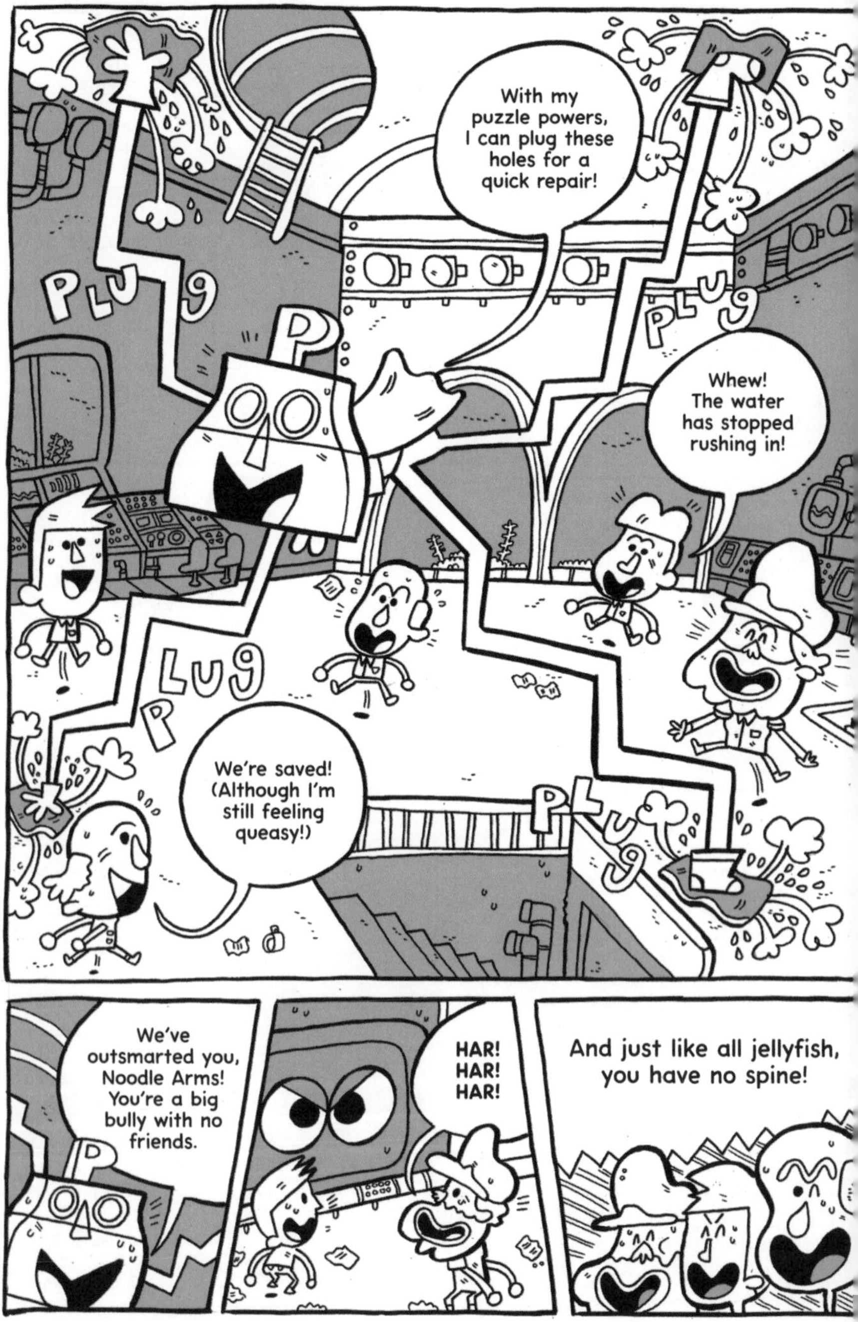
With my puzzle powers, I can plug these holes for a quick repair!
PLUG
PLUG
Whew! The water has stopped rushing in!
PLUG
We're saved! (Although I'm still feeling queasy!)
PLUG
We've outsmarted you, Noodle Arms! You're a big bully with no friends.
HAR! HAR! HAR!
And just like all jellyfish, you have no spine!

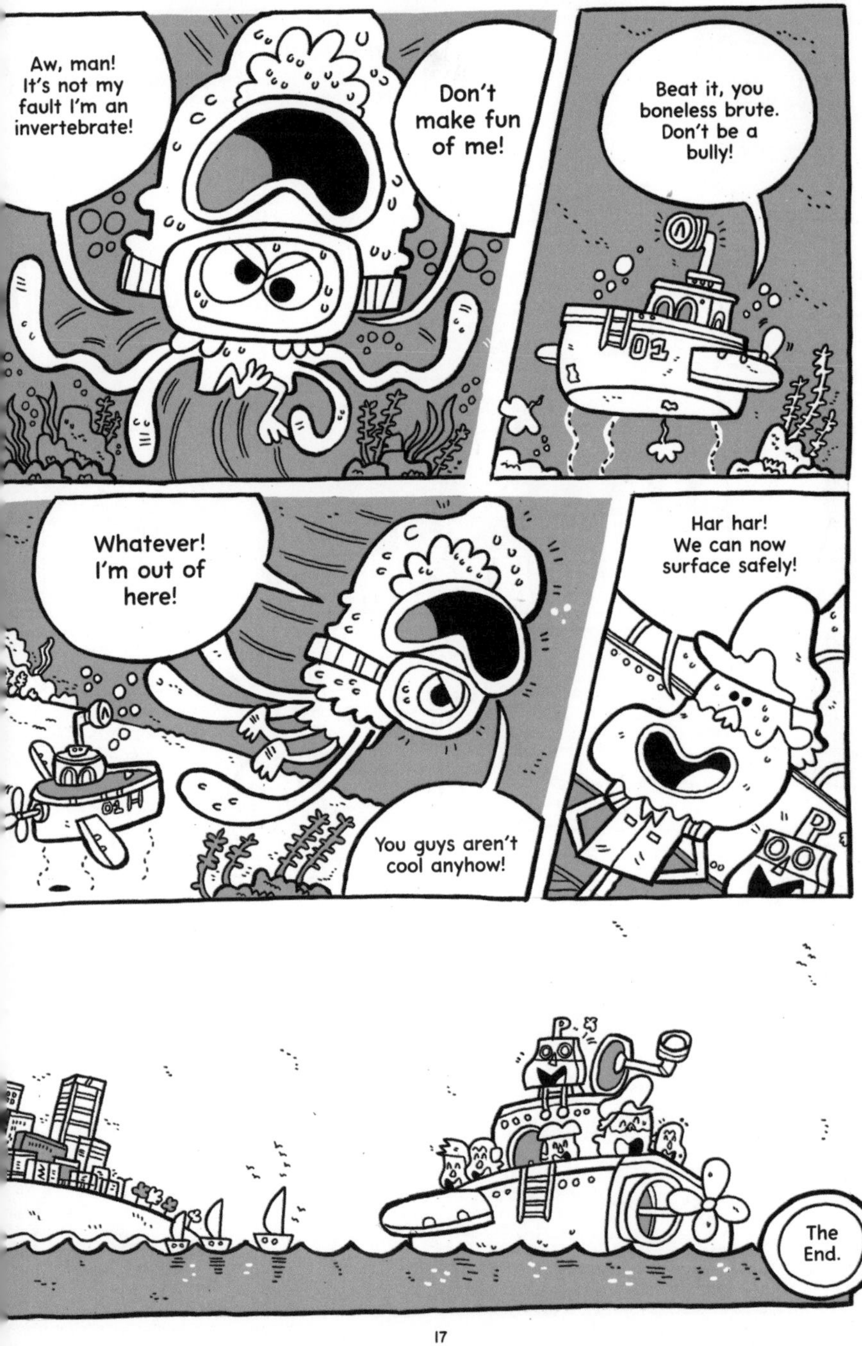
Aw, man! It's not my fault I'm an invertebrate!
Don't make fun of me!
Beat it, you boneless brute. Don't be a bully!
01
Whatever! I'm out of here!
01
You guys aren't cool anyhow!
Har har! We can now surface safely!
P
P
The End.

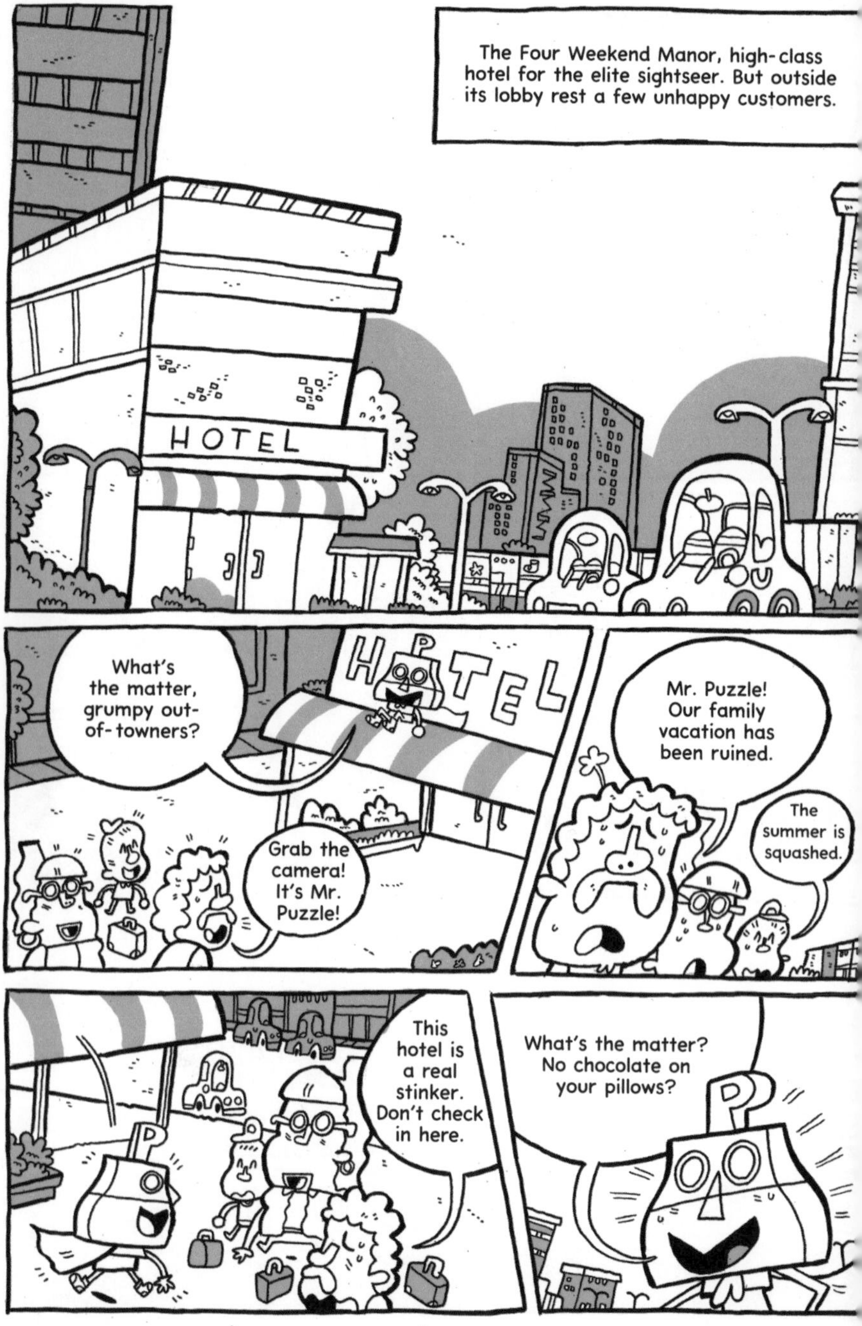
The Four Weekend Manor, high-class hotel for the elite sightseer. But outside its lobby rest a few unhappy customers.
HOTEL
What's the matter, grumpy out-of-towners?
Grab the camera! It's Mr. Puzzle!
Mr. Puzzle! Our family vacation has been ruined.
The summer is squashed.
This hotel is a real stinker. Don't check in here.
What's the matter? No chocolate on your pillows?

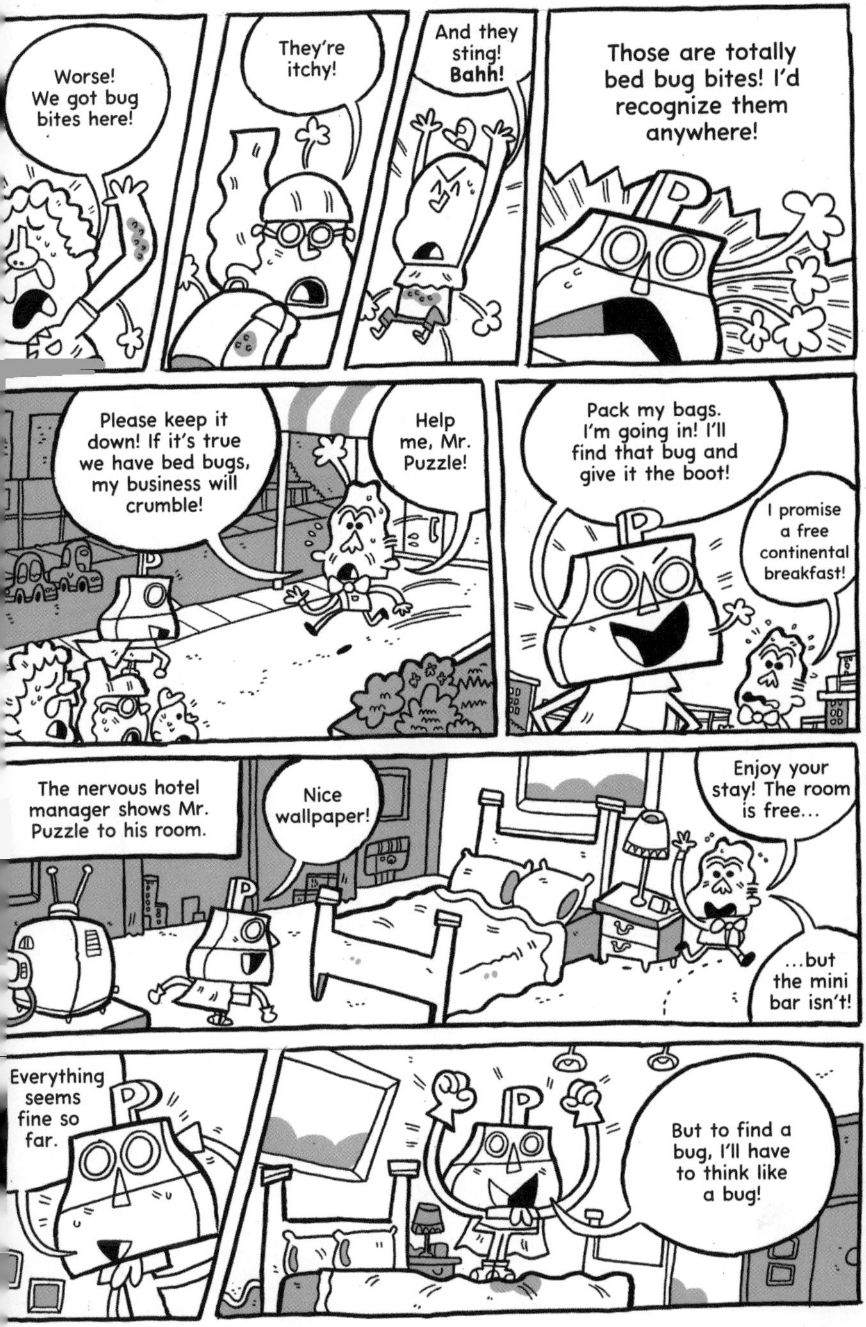
Worse! We got bug bites here!
They're itchy!
And they sting! Bahh!
Those are totally bed bug bites! I'd recognize them anywhere!
Please keep it down! If it's true we have bed bugs, my business will crumble!
Help me, Mr. Puzzle!
Pack my bags. I'm going in! I'll find that bug and give it the boot!
I promise a free continental breakfast!
The nervous hotel manager shows Mr. Puzzle to his room.
Nice wallpaper!
Enjoy your stay! The room is free...
...but the mini bar isn't!
Everything seems fine so far.
But to find a bug, I'll have to think like a bug!

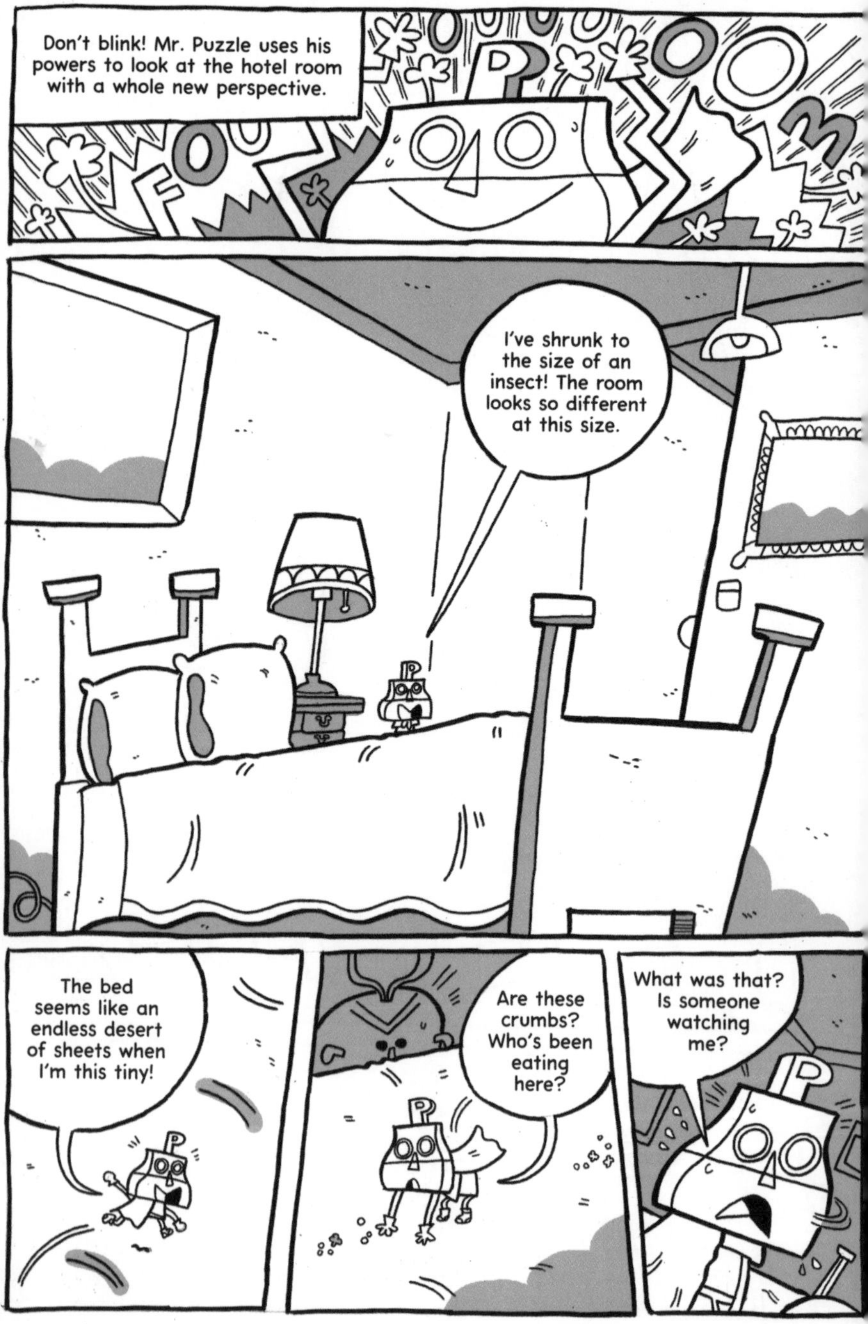
Don't blink! Mr. Puzzle uses his powers to look at the hotel room with a whole new perspective.
FOOOOOOOOM
I've shrunk to the size of an insect! The room looks so different at this size.
The bed seems like an endless desert of sheets when I'm this tiny!
Are these crumbs? Who's been eating here?
What was that? Is someone watching me?

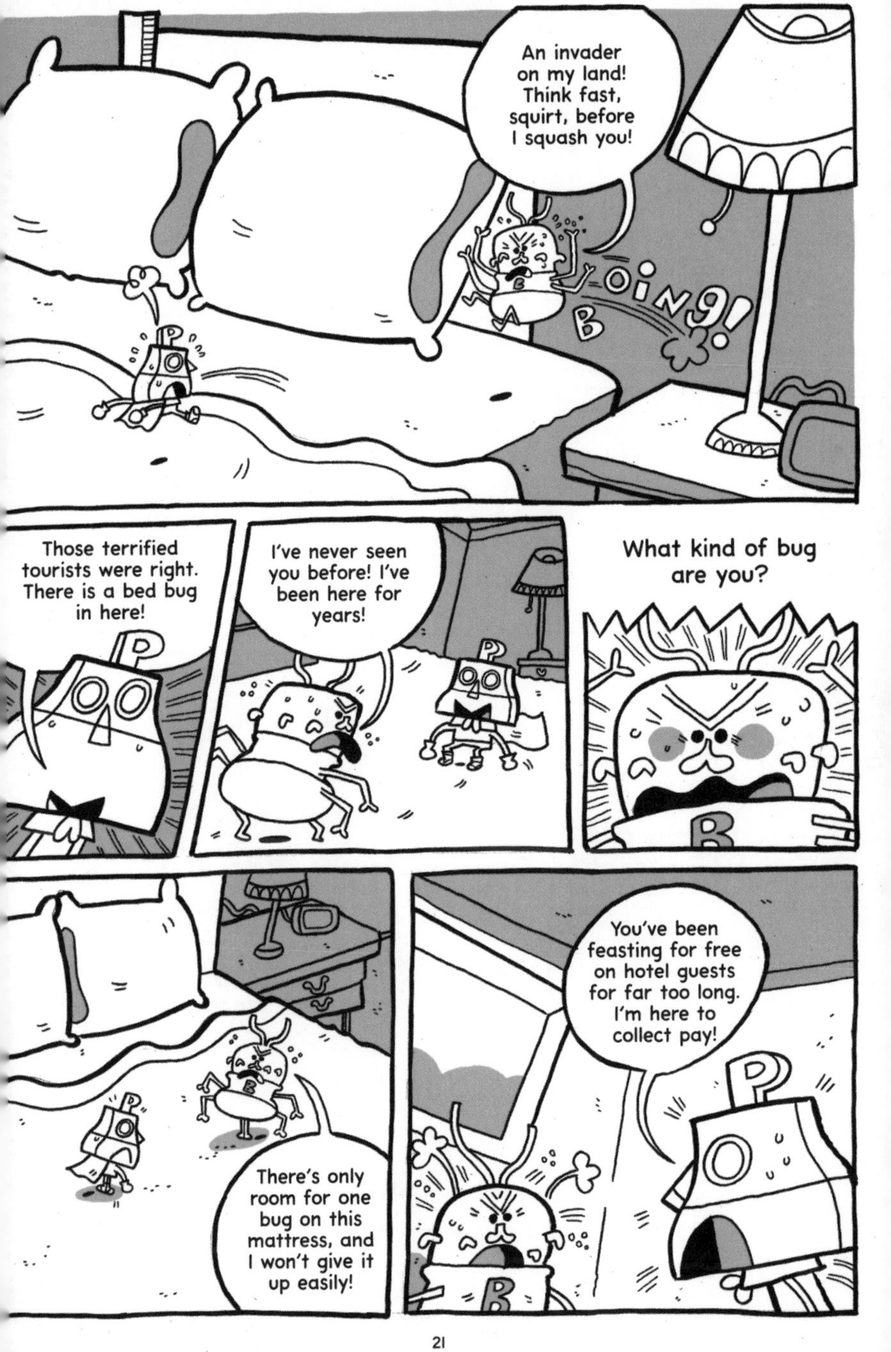

An invader on my land! Think fast, squirt, before I squash you!
BOING!
Those terrified tourists were right. There is a bed bug in here!
I've never seen you before! I've been here for years!
What kind of bug are you?
There's only room for one bug on this mattress, and I won't give it up easily!
You've been feasting for free on hotel guests for far too long. I'm here to collect pay!

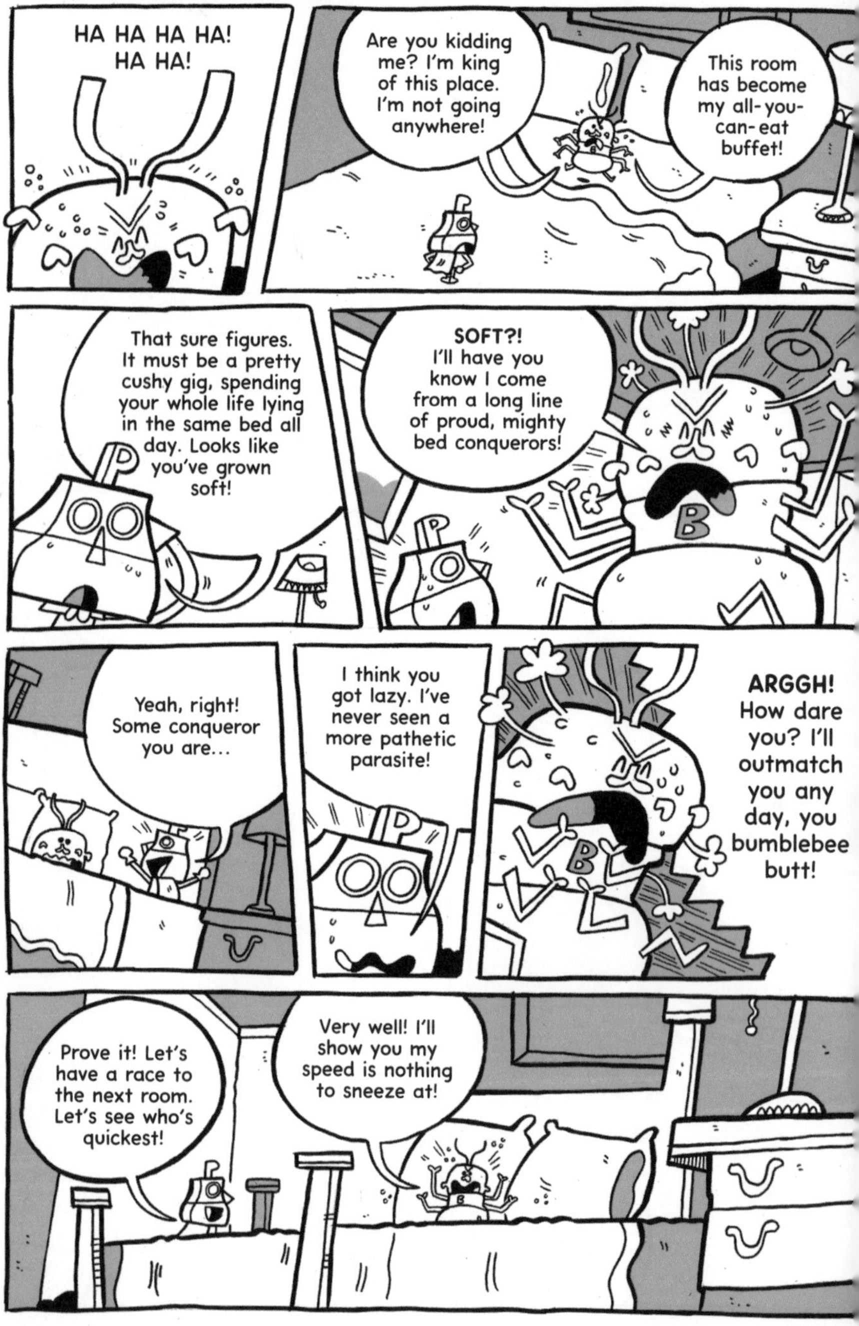
HA HA HA HA!
HA HA!
Are you kidding me? I'm king of this place. I'm not going anywhere!
This room has become my all-you-can-eat buffet!
That sure figures. It must be a pretty cushy gig, spending your whole life lying in the same bed all day. Looks like you've grown soft!
SOFT?! I'll have you know I come from a long line of proud, mighty bed conquerors!
Yeah, right! Some conqueror you are...
I think you got lazy. I've never seen a more pathetic parasite!
ARGGH! How dare you? I'll outmatch you any day, you bumblebee butt!
Prove it! Let's have a race to the next room. Let's see who's quickest!
Very well! I'll show you my speed is nothing to sneeze at!

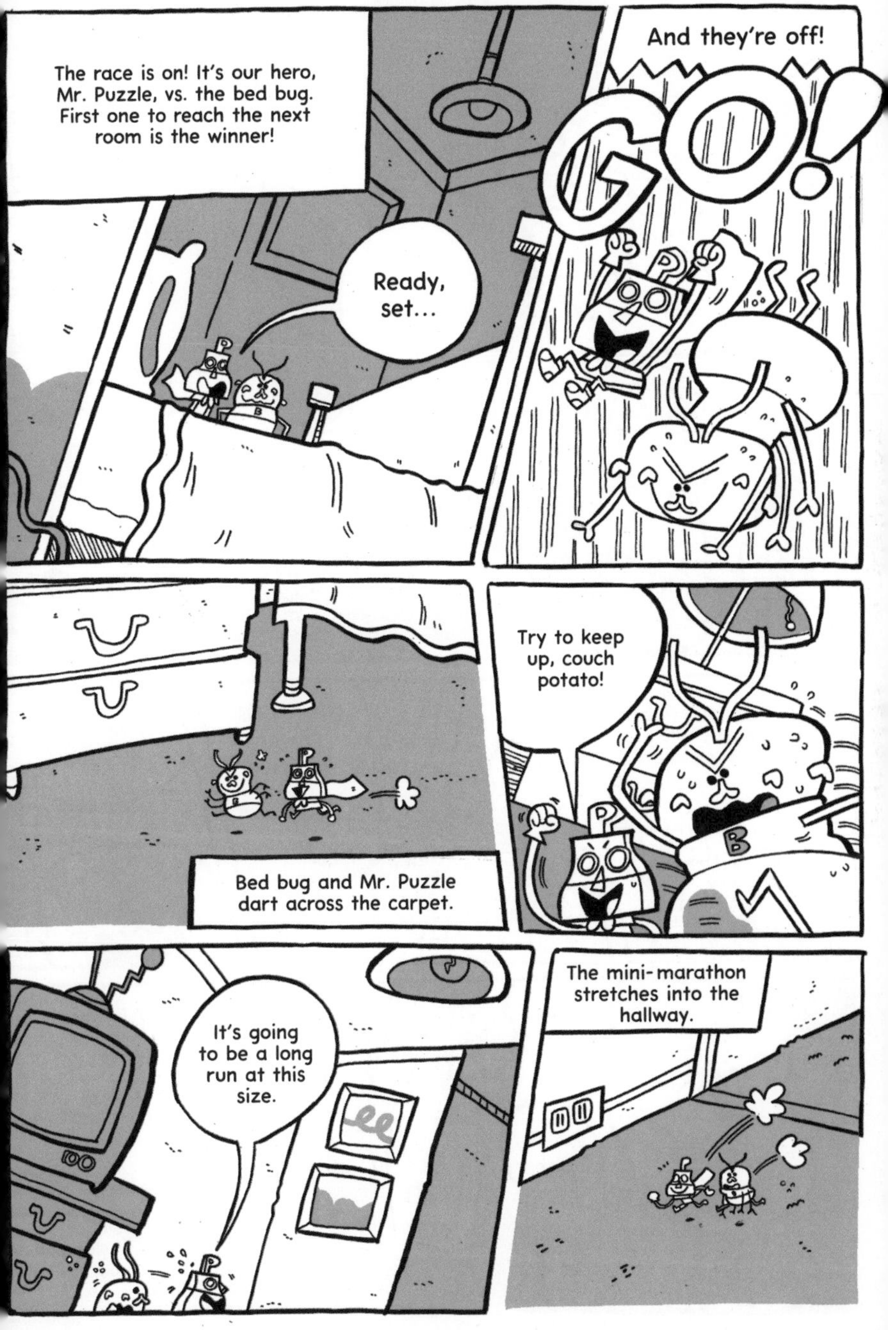

The race is on! It's our hero, Mr. Puzzle, vs. the bed bug. First one to reach the next room is the winner!
Ready, set...
And they're off!
GO!
Bed bug and Mr. Puzzle dart across the carpet.
Try to keep up, couch potato!
It's going to be a long run at this size.
The mini-marathon stretches into the hallway.

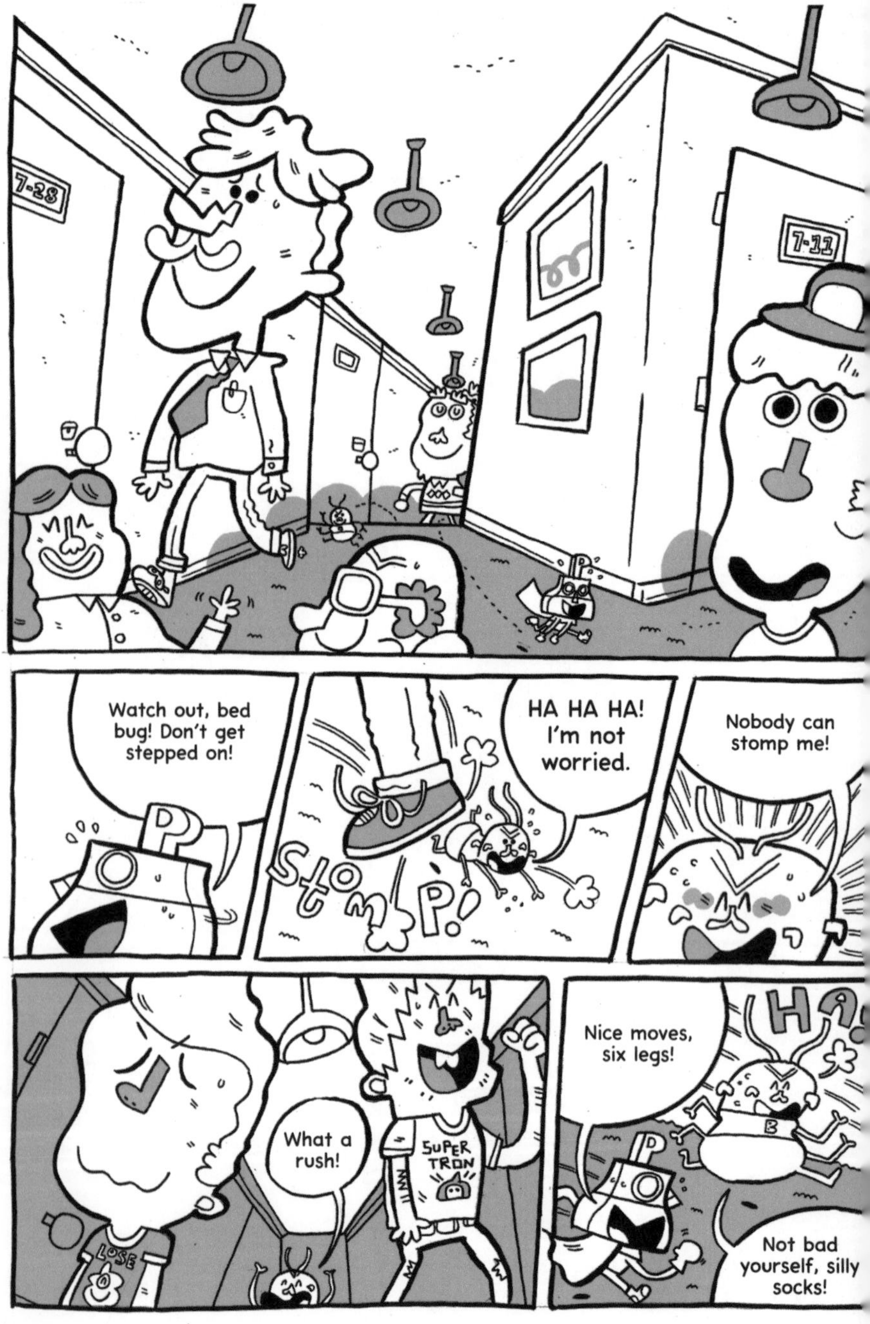
7-28
7-11
Watch out, bed bug! Don't get stepped on!
STOMP!
HA HA HA! I'm not worried.
Nobody can stomp me!
What a rush!
SUPER TRON
LOSE
Nice moves, six legs!
HA
B
Not bad yourself, silly socks!

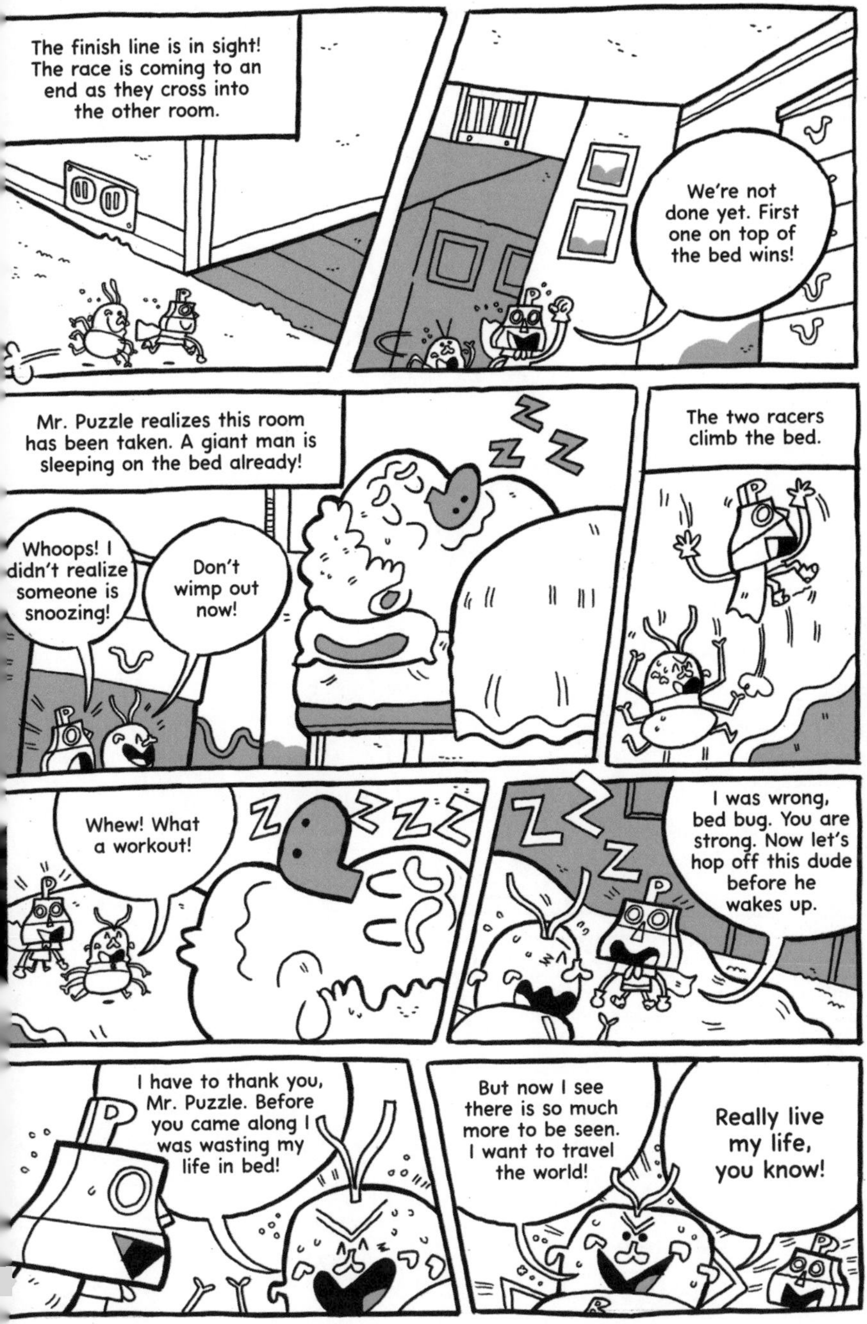
The finish line is in sight! The race is coming to an end as they cross into the other room.
We're not done yet. First one on top of the bed wins!
Mr. Puzzle realizes this room has been taken. A giant man is sleeping on the bed already!
Whoops! I didn't realize someone is snoozing!
Don't wimp out now!
The two racers climb the bed.
Whew! What a workout!
I was wrong, bed bug. You are strong. Now let's hop off this dude before he wakes up.
I have to thank you, Mr. Puzzle. Before you came along I was wasting my life in bed!
But now I see there is so much more to be seen. I want to travel the world!
Really live my life, you know!

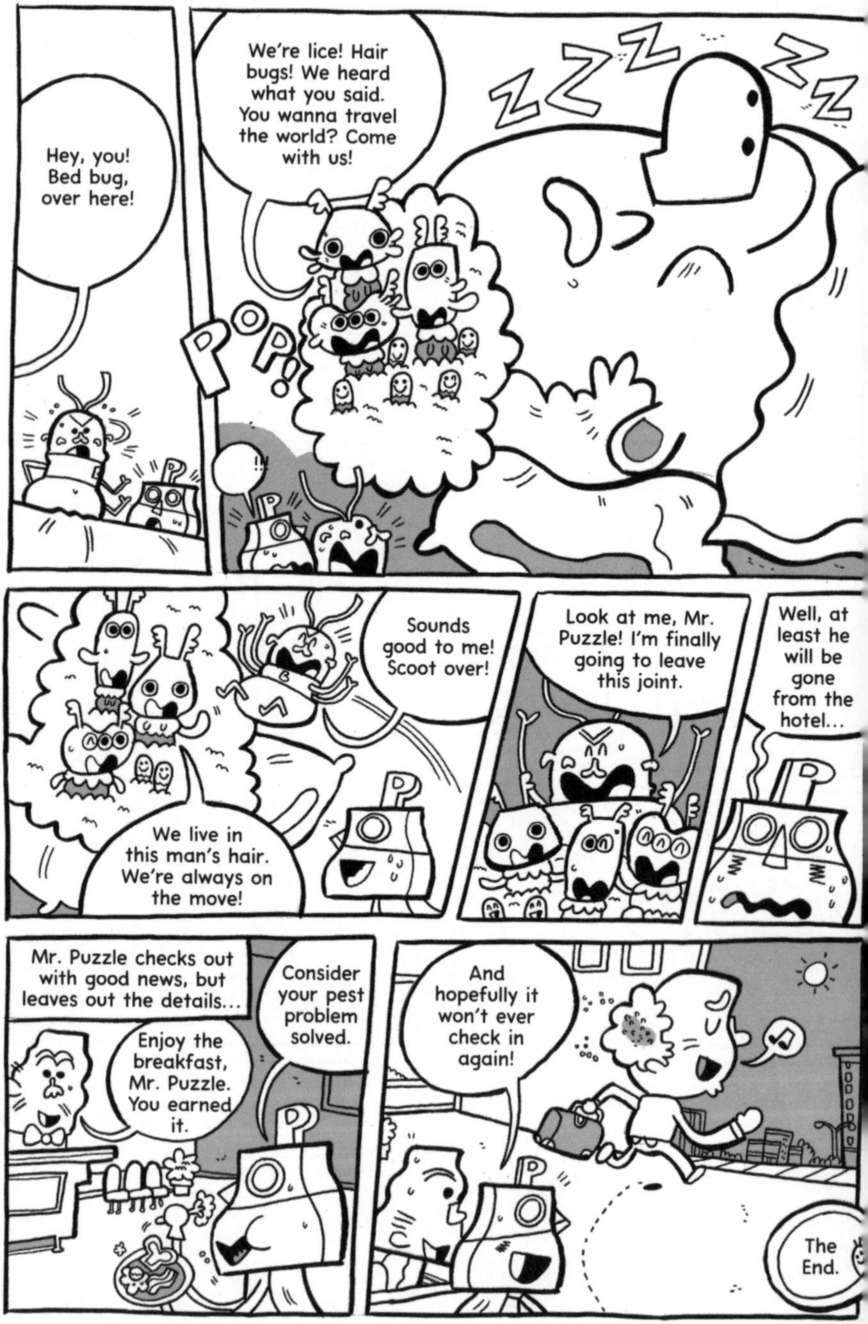
Hey, you! Bed bug, over here!
We're lice! Hair bugs! We heard what you said. You wanna travel the world? Come with us!
ZZZZZZ
POP!
!!!
Sounds good to me! Scoot over!
We live in this man's hair. We're always on the move!
Look at me, Mr. Puzzle! I'm finally going to leave this joint.
Well, at least he will be gone from the hotel...
Mr. Puzzle checks out with good news, but leaves out the details...
Enjoy the breakfast, Mr. Puzzle. You earned it.
Consider your pest problem solved.
And hopefully it won't ever check in again!
The End.

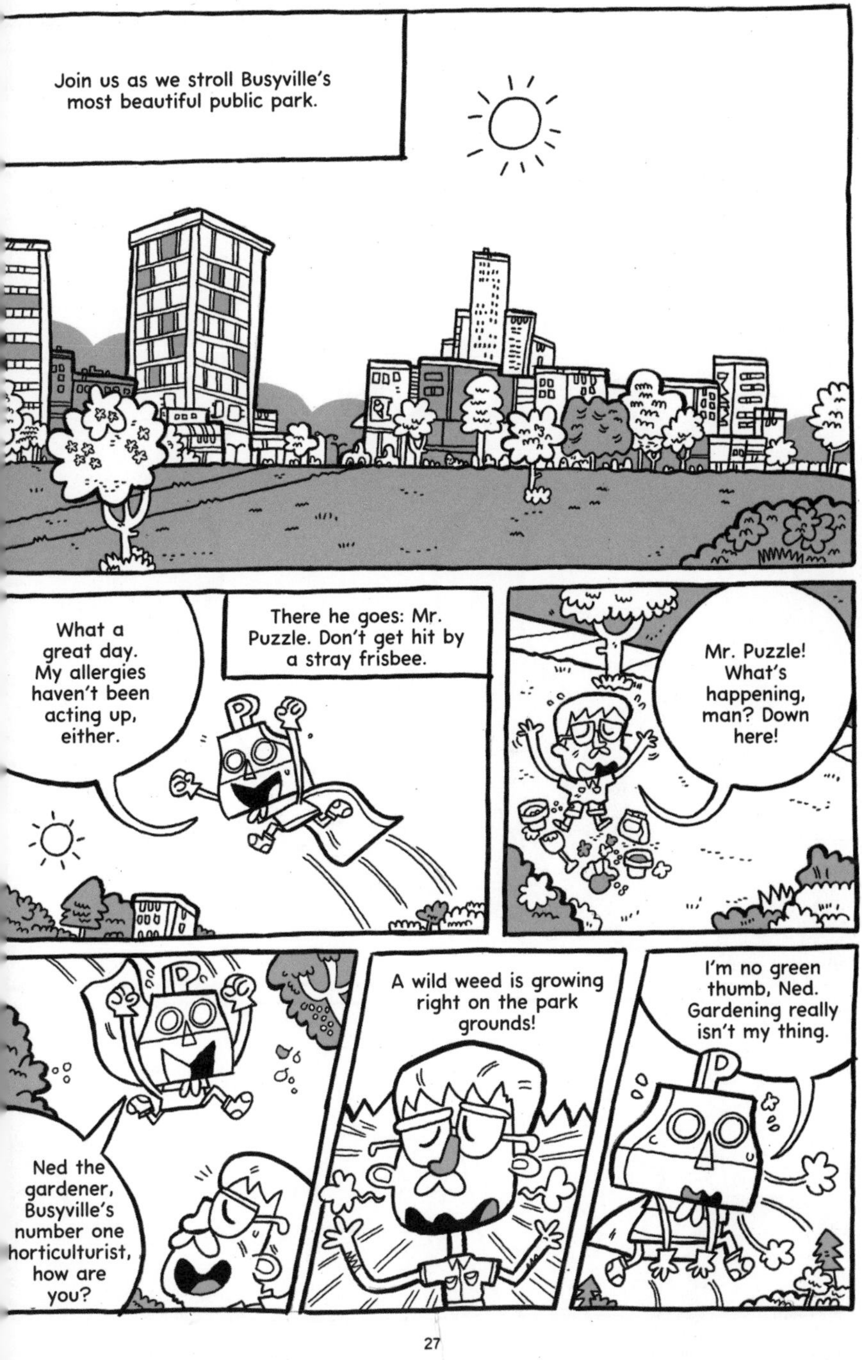

Join us as we stroll Busyville's most beautiful public park.
What a great day. My allergies haven't been acting up, either.
There he goes: Mr. Puzzle. Don't get hit by a stray frisbee.
Mr. Puzzle! What's happening, man? Down here!
Ned the gardener, Busyville's number one horticulturist, how are you?
A wild weed is growing right on the park grounds!
I'm no green thumb, Ned. Gardening really isn't my thing.

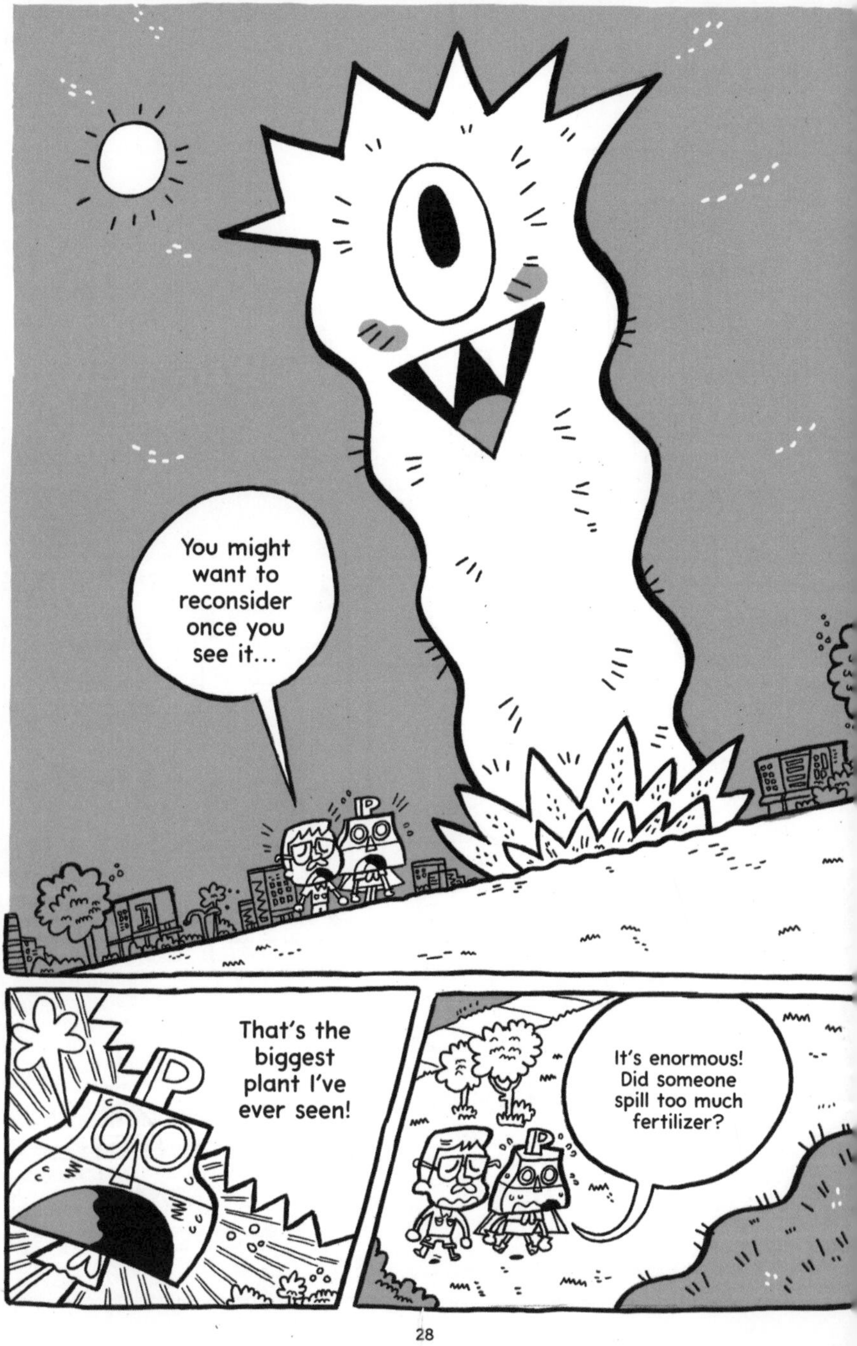
You might want to reconsider once you see it...
That's the biggest plant I've ever seen!
It's enormous! Did someone spill too much fertilizer?

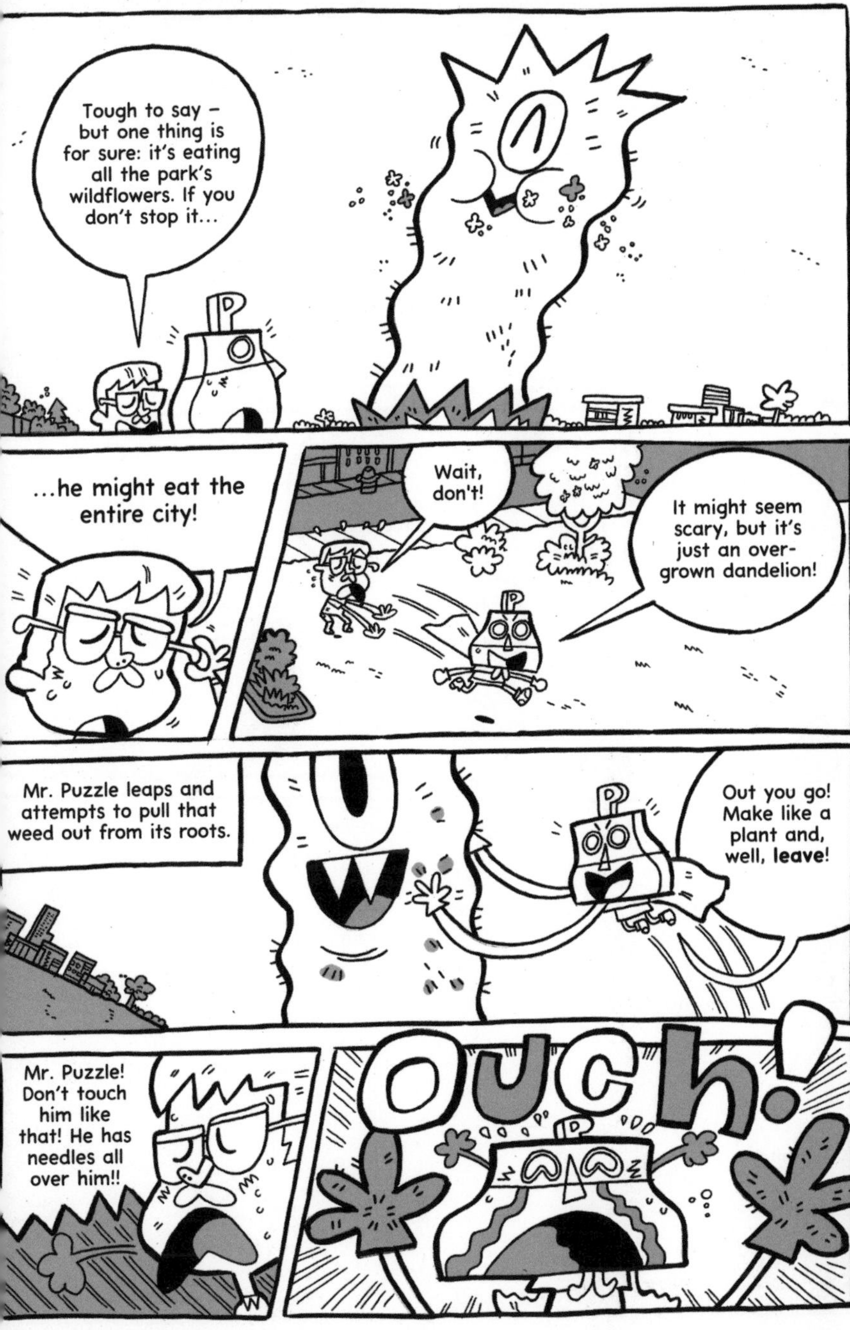

Tough to say – but one thing is for sure: it's eating all the park's wildflowers. If you don't stop it...
...he might eat the entire city!
Wait, don't!
It might seem scary, but it's just an over-grown dandelion!
Mr. Puzzle leaps and attempts to pull that weed out from its roots.
Out you go! Make like a plant and, well, **leave**!
Mr. Puzzle! Don't touch him like that! He has needles all over him!!
Ouch!

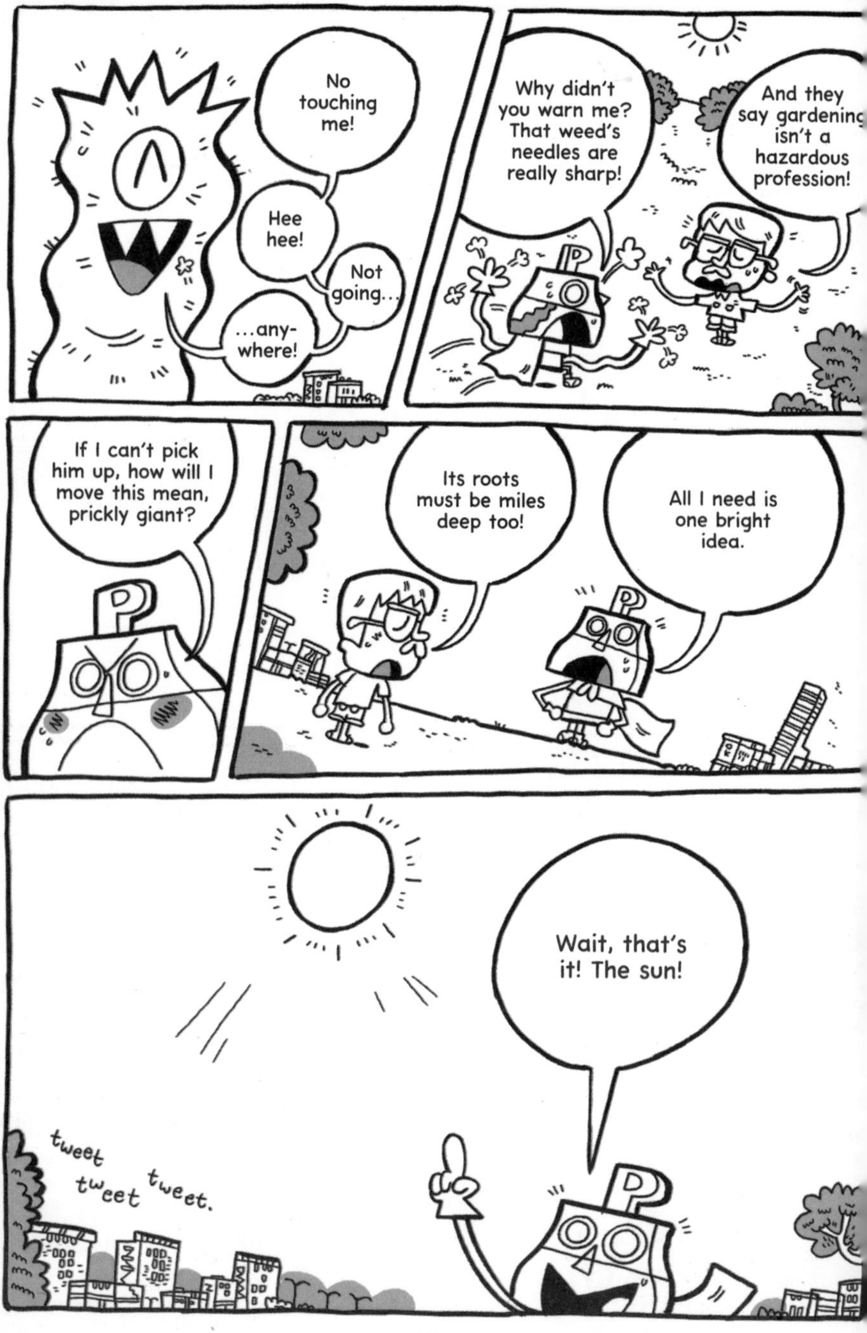

No touching me!
Hee hee!
Not going...
...any-where!
Why didn't you warn me? That weed's needles are really sharp!
And they say gardening isn't a hazardous profession!
If I can't pick him up, how will I move this mean, prickly giant?
Its roots must be miles deep too!
All I need is one bright idea.
Wait, that's it! The sun!
tweet tweet tweet.

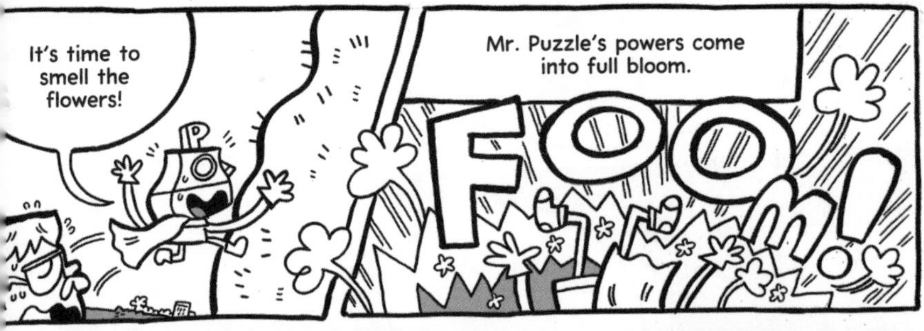
It's time to smell the flowers!
Mr. Puzzle's powers come into full bloom.
FOOM!

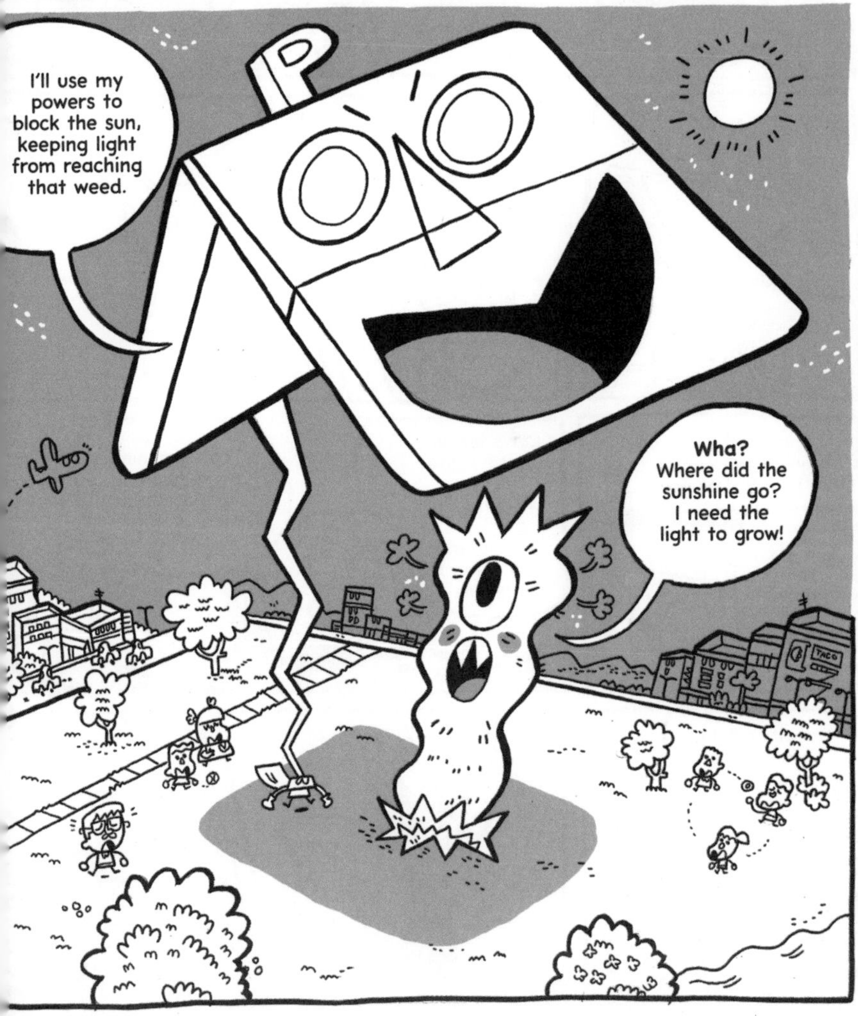
I'll use my powers to block the sun, keeping light from reaching that weed.
Wha? Where did the sunshine go? I need the light to grow!
TACO

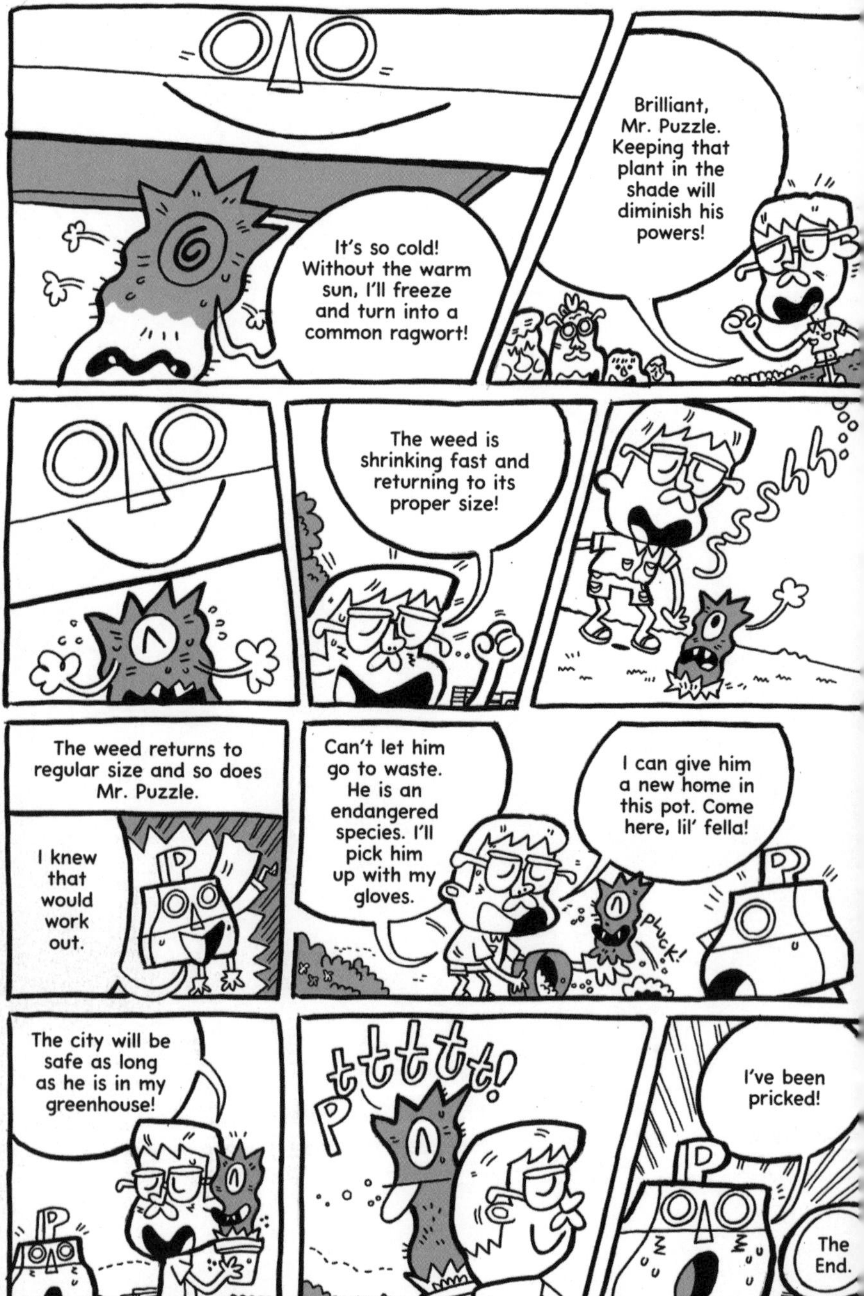
It's so cold! Without the warm sun, I'll freeze and turn into a common ragwort!
Brilliant, Mr. Puzzle. Keeping that plant in the shade will diminish his powers!
The weed is shrinking fast and returning to its proper size!
sssshhh
The weed returns to regular size and so does Mr. Puzzle.
I knew that would work out.
Can't let him go to waste. He is an endangered species. I'll pick him up with my gloves.
I can give him a new home in this pot. Come here, lil' fella!
PLUCK!
The city will be safe as long as he is in my greenhouse!
Ptttttt!
I've been pricked!
The End.

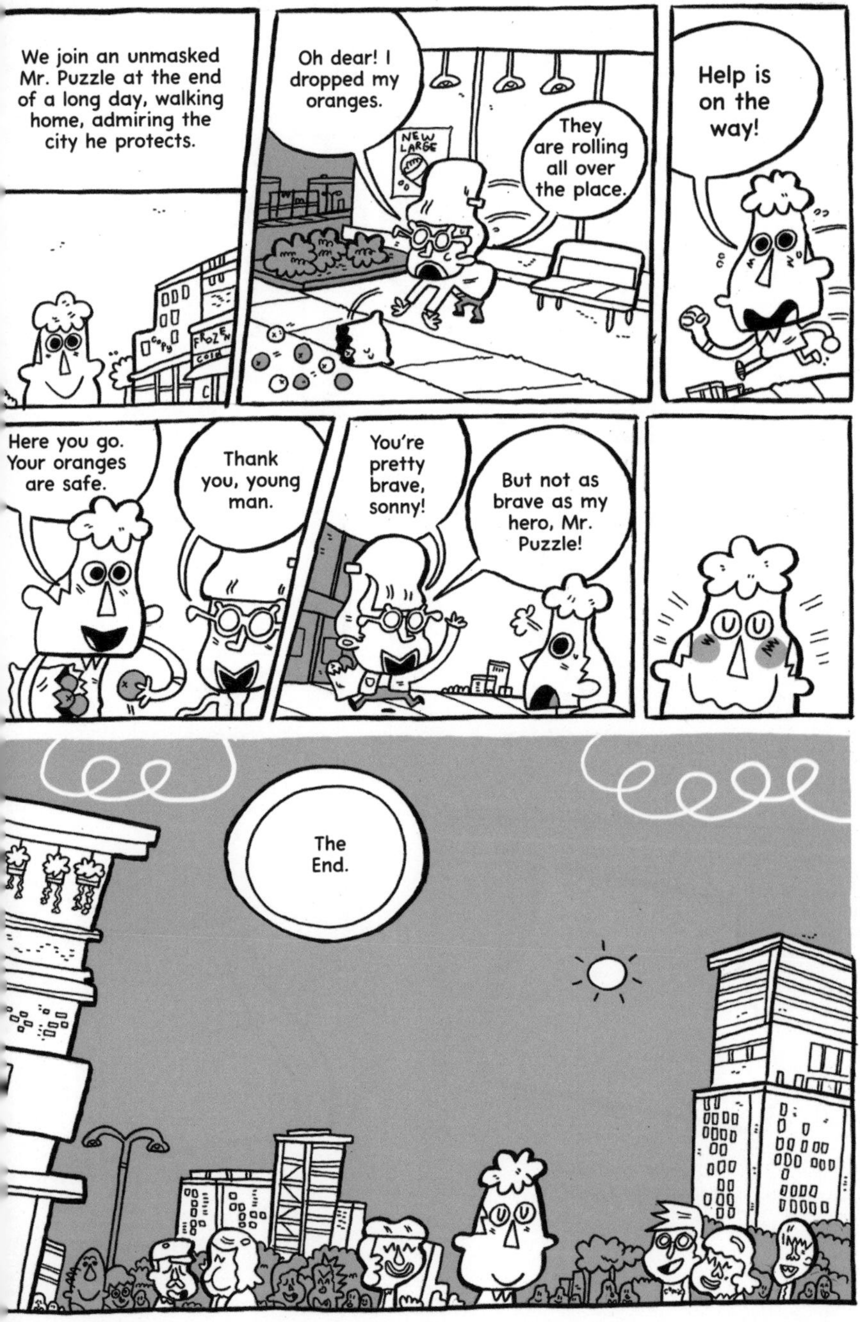
We join an unmasked Mr. Puzzle at the end of a long day, walking home, admiring the city he protects.
Copy
FROZEN
Cold
Oh dear! I dropped my oranges.
NEW LARGE
They are rolling all over the place.
Help is on the way!
Here you go. Your oranges are safe.
Thank you, young man.
You're pretty brave, sonny!
But not as brave as my hero, Mr. Puzzle!
The End.

HOW TO DRAW

You'll need:

A Pencil!

Some Paper!

I.

Draw a shape similar to this.

2.

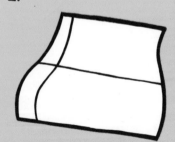

Remember Mr. Puzzle needs some dimension.

3.

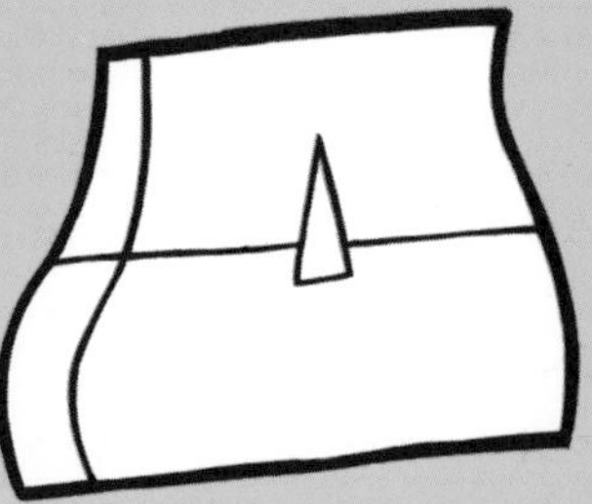

A pointy triangle works great for his nose.

4.

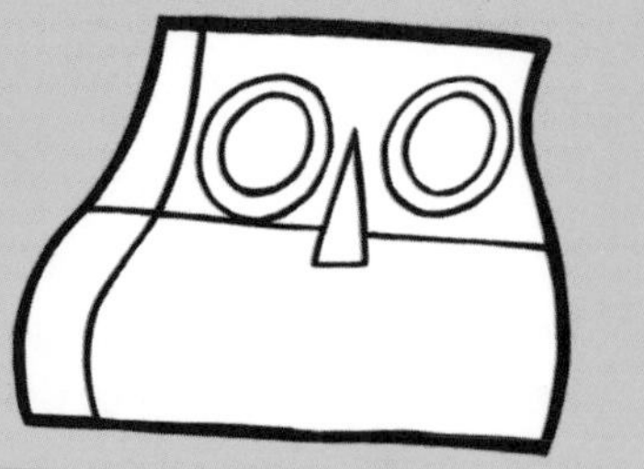

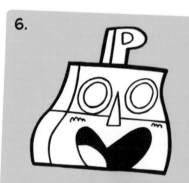

Add some circles for eyes!

5.

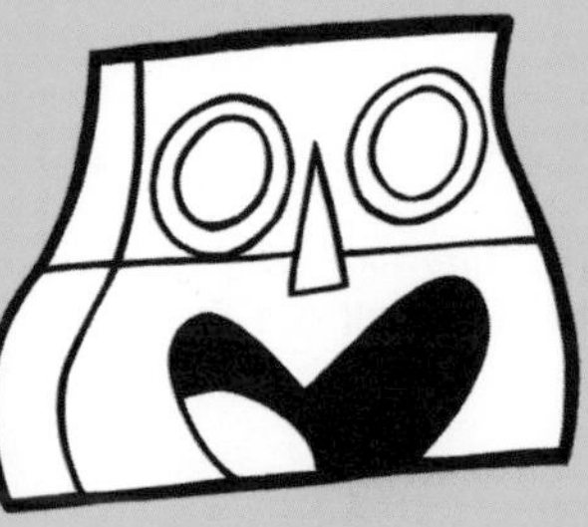

Of course he needs a mouth!

6.

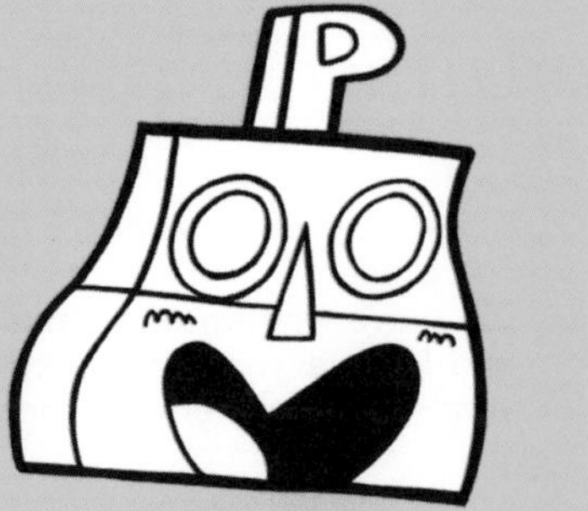

We can't forget Mr. Puzzle's "P" and rosy cheeks!

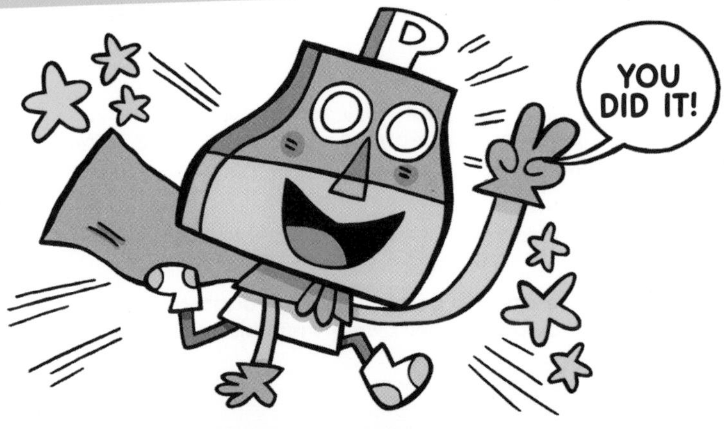
YOU DID IT!

CREATOR

CHRIS ELIOPOULOS is a professional illustrator and cartoonist from Chicago! He is also an adjunct professor at Columbia College Chicago in the art and design department. He is the writer and artist on several all-ages graphic novels and series: *Okie Dokie Donuts* published by Top Shelf; *Gabba Ball!* published by Oni Press; and *Monster Party* published by Koyama Press. OTHER clients include Disney Animation Studios, Yo Gabba Gabba!, Nick Jr., Cloudkid, and Simon and Schuster.

Q & A

What has been your favorite part of the book or character to tackle?
CE: I love writing and making up bad guys. They like to shout and let everyone know why they are upset. They all act like two-year-olds with temper tantrums.

Why should people read Mr. Puzzle?
CE: It's a lot of fun, totally silly, and lighthearted. If this comic book were food, it would be a bag of gummy bears.

What's your favorite part about working in comics?
CE: Drawing all day long!

What was the first comic you remember reading?
CE: The Super Mario Adventures inside every issue of *Nintendo Power Magazine*.

Tell us why everyone should read comic books!

CE: What else are you going to read? Furniture assembly instructions or dishwasher owner manuals—yuck!

GLOSSARY

abandon (uh-BAN-duhn)—to leave forever

allergic (uh-LUR-jik)—affected by something that causes you to sneeze, get a rash, or have another reaction

barnacle (BAR-nuh-kuhl)—a small shellfish that attaches itself firmly to the side of boats or rocks

conqueror (KONG-kur-ur)—one who defeats an enemy

deceive (di-SEEV)—to lie, trick, or mislead

encore (ON-kor)—a demand made by an audience for a repeat or an additional performance

invertebrate (in-VUR-tuh-brit)—an animal (like a worm, clam, spider, or butterfly) that lacks a backbone

lice (LISSE)—small insects without wings that live on animals or people

paralyze (PA-ruh-lize)—to make something helpless or unable to function

parasite (PA-ruh-site)—an animal or plant that gets its food by living on or inside another animal or plant

pyrotechnics (py-roh-TEK-nikz)—a display of fireworks

queasy (KWEE-zee)—sick to your stomach

zombie (ZOM-bee)—a person has died and been brought back to life

MR. PUZZLE
BRAIN BENDERS!

1. Mr. Puzzle got his superpowers from an ancient puzzle. Imagine you are a superhero. Write a paragraph about how you gained superpowers.

2. Who is your favorite villain in this book – the Mint Chocolate Zombies, the giant jellyfish, the bed bug, or the prickly plant? Explain your answer using an example from the story.

3. Mr. Puzzle is really Walter, a super smart guy. Write a paragraph what you think Walter does when he's not Mr. Puzzle. Is Walter married? Does he have kids? What kind of job does he have?

4. Write a song for the Mint Chocolate Zombies. What would this gruesome band sing about? You decide!

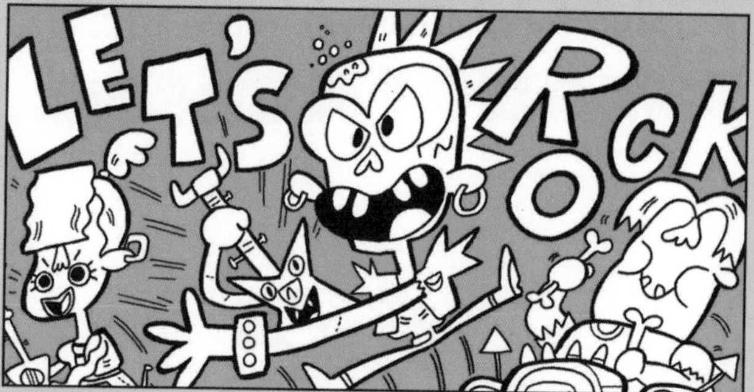
LET'S ROCK

5. On page 26, the bed bug leaves the hotel, but he has now joined a pesky gang of lice. Do you think Mr. Puzzle is happy with this solution? Why or why not?

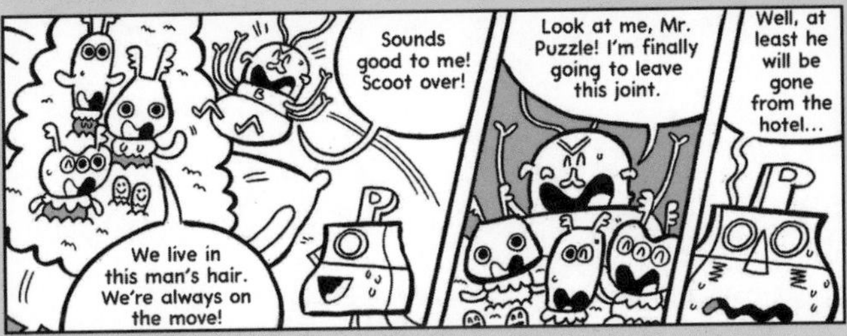
We live in this man's hair. We're always on the move!
Sounds good to me! Scoot over!
Look at me, Mr. Puzzle! I'm finally going to leave this joint.
Well, at least he will be gone from the hotel...

6. On page 31, Mr. Puzzle defeats the giant plant by blocking out the sun. Describe at least two other ways Mr. Puzzle could have stopped this prickly problem.

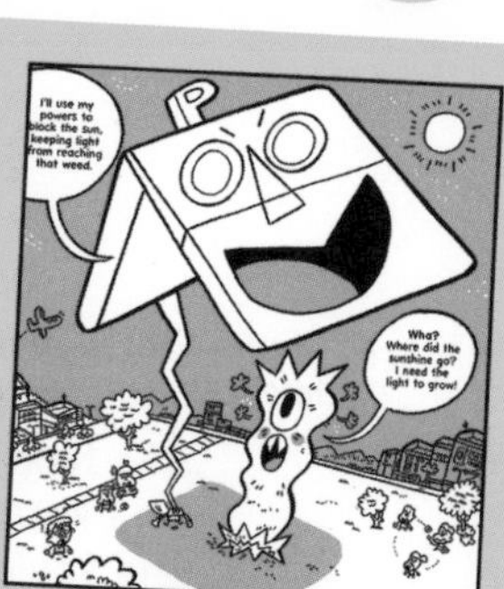
I'll use my powers to block the sun, keeping light from reaching that weed.
Wha? Where did the sunshine go? I need the light to grow!

The **Mr. PUZZLE** fun doesn't
stop here! Discover more at...

WWW.CAPSTONEKIDS.COM

Find cool websites and more books
like this one at **www.facthound.com**

Just type in the Book ID:
9781434260253
And you're ready to go!